WHITE COAT AND SNEAKERS
A NOVEL

BY

HILLARY CHOLLET, M.D.

COPYRIGHT 2012

Author's Note

White Coat and Sneakers is a novel based on the life and family of Hillary A.P. Chollet–born July 25, 1926. All other characters appearing in this work are fictitious. Any resemblance to real persons, living or dead, is purely coincidental.

This novel is dedicated to my dad Hillary Sr., his brother Leroy, and my cousin Eric. Each one had Lou Gehrig's disease—ALS. History will support they tried their best in life.

ACKNOWLEDGEMENT

A special thanks to my wife Maureen for her loving support and spiritual guidance.

CHAPTER 1

⚬⚬⚬

As my head hits the pillow, I let out a sigh of relief. This is my thirty-eighth straight hour without sleep. My call room is in a trailer in a parking lot attached to CGH—a world-renowned medical and trauma center in Los Angeles.

It's difficult to find words to describe this "home away from home." Tissue-paper-thin walls are complemented by a broken lampshade, an old desktop computer, and a TV with only three working channels. The relentless drone of freeway traffic right next door hits my eardrums and then bounces off the backs of my eyes before concussing off my frontal lobes. Numerous boluses of caffeine, along with lack of sleep, have triggered a triad of feelings: dizziness, a pounding heart that makes a sound like horses running down the back stretch at the Kentucky Derby, and the same physical and mental aches I get when hitting mile twenty of a marathon.

It's 1:00 a.m. Call finishes in six hours. I'm barely able to keep my eyes open but unable to keep them closed because of multiple racing thoughts; an aura of delirium develops. While I stare at the ceiling, a bug comes into focus. A feeling of envy washes through my mind as I watch this six-legged black dot slowly crawl toward the corner. Doesn't seem like he's under any pressure, no high expectations—he can walk upside down and seems to be able to rest anytime he wants. Am I going crazy? Am I psychotic?

The bug makes it to its destination and disappears quietly into the night. Inside this ten-foot-by-ten-foot tin box, I rest and stare at the ceiling with my open eyes, trying to find the switch that will turn off the racing thoughts that have been hyper-charged by this no-sleep marathon. With eyes closed, I say my prayers.

"Dear God, thank you for taking care of me. Please bless my dad, who, as a surgeon, has helped many people but now has Lou Gehrig's disease. Also bless my mom in heaven."

This reflection allows my eyes to grow very heavy, and I fall asleep.

Perhaps fifteen minutes later a shrill *beep, beep, beep* goes off. The pager on the nightstand takes on a life of its own. It only makes two sounds—the *beep, beep, beep* when it goes off and a slightly different beep when its battery runs low. What an existence it has—to rudely make its sound whenever it wants and then expect me to feed it (change its battery) whenever it wants. A blue-lit screen reads "707-6." Within seconds, my other pager chirps. Another "707-6." Next, the trauma phone rings.

"Hello, Dr. Chollet," says the shrill voice of a secretary. "We have a trauma arriving in six minutes."

Finally my personal cell phone rings, and it's the hospital operator. "Dr. Chollet, we have a trauma coming in six minutes."

Since I was sleeping in my scrubs already, I put on my socks, one inside out, and step into a pair of old New Balance sneaks. Quietly the words "Holy shit" pop out without apparent reason. In my attempt to wake up, I splash water from the bathroom faucet onto my face and neck. Staring in the mirror over the sink and barely recognizing the person staring back, I conclude this has to be a homeless person in scrubs; I'm unshaven, with partially combed, long black hair with a few flecks of gray. "Already? At thirty-two years old? Great!"

I'm half-hoping my trauma patient arrives unconscious, because there's no way a sane awake patient could keep a straight face when he or she saw me.

Out the trailer, down three steps, white coat, stethoscope, beepers, and phones all in tow, a new energy emerges that awakens the actions necessary for clarity, calm, and "quiet eyes."

After pressing Hoku points, I complete my transformation. I reach for my ID badge and keyless key, and then ponder the picture and the info on the badge: name, rank, and serial number. Hillary A. A. Chollet, MD, FACS, Trauma Vascular surgeon, doctor #1840.

Is there additional info on that magnetic card—maybe one's often-mentioned but never seen "permanent record"?

Entering the hospital with a single swipe of the ID badge, I review my hospital strategy.

Three rules:

1) Anything you say can and will be used against you.

2) No good deed goes unpunished.

3) Nice guys finish last.

The hospital itself is a monolithic entity without a heart or conscience. Full of rules and administrative mandates, the hospital is not on the side of the doctor or the patient. It is on its own side.

After entering, one sees a long corridor with bright lights, dingy walls with no artwork, and no sign of keeping up with the times. As I approach an intersection, out pops Janelle, a slim, dark-haired, twenty-two-year-old, very smart third year medical student. She's nice looking with blue eyes and offers the faintest smell of jasmine perfume. She asks, "What do we have?"

Walking quickly, we are met by Henry, the surgery resident, who, having overheard, answers Janelle's question. "It's a shooting—a young kid with barely any vital signs."

"707-6" is how the page came across. "707" signifies a high-level, life-threatening trauma. "707" stands for the letters that accompany numbers on a phone pad; it translates to "SOS" or "Save our souls." "–6" means "Arrival in six minutes."

Henry also has been up for nearly forty hours, but still in his twenties, he has good stamina. A big muscular fellow, nearly six-two and 225 pounds, good looking, with blond hair and black glasses, he was told to go into orthopedics. Last year in the ICU, he changed his mind after cracking the chest of some lady who had ruptured an aortic aneurysm. Luckily he got her heart started again and called me, and we were able to fix things and pull her through. She went home on Thanksgiving Day. After that, Henry was like a little puppy dog with his new family—no longer the ortho family, now the trauma vascular surgery family.

Approaching the trauma room, we see the usual gallery of looky-loos hoping to get a glimpse of the potential carnage. Upon entering this twenty-by-twenty foyer of life and death via an internal corridor door, we are met by two L.A. Fire Department paramedics entering from the opposite side of the room and hurriedly pushing a stretcher. I jump into action with my usual greeting. "Hi, guys. What do we have here?"

Paramedics create order from disorder. Within the trauma room, there is a cadre of people along with the pulse of panic. Sometimes they work like a well-oiled machine and sometimes like the Tin Man in *The Wizard of Oz*—not so well oiled. This orchestra of providers includes an anesthesia doctor, an emergency doctor, a representative from pastoral care, a nurse for the right side of the patient, a nurse for the left side of the patient, an X-ray tech, a CAT scan tech, and a person from the front desk who is a clerk waiting to ask the patient what kind of insurance he has.

As the de facto maestro or captain of the ship, I feel this is going to be a Tin Man situation—too much panic and tension. The paramedic gives his report. "Doc, I have a sixteen-year-old male who was shot twice in the belly about seventeen minutes ago. He was briefly awake and alert. About five minutes ago he lost his pressure, and we were barely able to even feel a pulse."

First I ask myself, *Is this young man going to live one more minute without my doing something extreme to save him?* Answer: *Yes.* Next question: *Will he live five minutes?* Answer: *No!* We've got big trouble. In trauma it goes A, airway; B, breathing; C, circulation; D, disability; and E, environment/exposure.

After we secure an **A**irway with a breathing tube down his throat into his windpipe, I listen with my stethoscope and hear a barely perceptible heartbeat. I'm happy to hear equal **B**reath sounds, and then my hand goes to feel for a pulse in his groin. At most it's a thready pulse that's difficult to feel, revealing a **C**irculation problem. Shock from blood loss causes all of the blood vessels to constrict except the ones to the brain and heart—a variant of the mammalian diving reflex.

Dolphins have mastered this, but only the youngest of humans can muster such a response when cold or in trauma. Feeling with the tips of my fingers for his femoral artery in the left groin, I again feel the barely perceptible pulse. If this cord of arterial constriction were one of the strings of a violin, when plucked it would utter the D-major sound of a cry for help—a sound heard when one is close to clinical death. With such a dire presentation, I make an immediate decision to go straight to the operating room. Out comes the trauma phone; I call the OR.

"Dr. Chollet here, warm the room to ninety degrees. We'll be in the OR with my patient in three minutes. Begin the massive transfusion protocol, and call in the cell-saver tech."

An inspection of this young man reveals that he is very thin. The nurses remove his shoes and his clothes are cut off. Still in socks,

I look at his right foot and see two dime-sized holes in his sock. As the humanity of this situation sets in, I feel like crying. A tingle goes up my spine and I am reminded that I must remain strong. Interestingly he does not have any tattoos. A quick exam shows what appear to be two large-caliber gunshot wounds to the abdomen. No exit points on a full turn and inspection of the back. A chest X-ray shows no retained bullets. An X-ray of the abdomen reveals two bullets in the lower quadrant. Ultrasound shows minimal cardiac activity. Within two or three minutes, the patient arrives in the operating room, where it is an entirely different circumstance.

There is at least some degree of panic, with nurses getting ready and blood being brought into the room, but definitely this is my area, where things are much calmer. Once on the OR table, the patient is prepped with a sterile soap from his chin to mid-thighs. With his profoundly low blood pressure, and signs of shock and internal blood loss, it is apparent to me that this sixteen-year-old male assault victim won't make it another minute if I don't do something extreme.

"Give me a knife" comes out just as the scrub nurse anticipates and slaps a number-twenty-two scalpel into the palm of my hand. This is followed by a generous incision over the left fifth rib—skin and everything straight through muscle down to the rib.

The left chest is entered, and a probing finger feels the barely beating heart. It is necessary to place a chest retractor between ribs four and five. Akin to the Jaws of Life, this retractor has a handle that is turned; this causes the chest to crank open, creating a hole big enough for a hand to be placed to work on the heart.

Experience tells me I only have thirty seconds or so or this kid is going to box—die. I quickly crank open the chest and hear the sound of cracking ribs. Similar to the sound of walnuts being cracked open, the noise sends chills down my spine. After I create an opening, I instinctively reach into the chest, fingers first, using the spine as my landmark. My fingers travel to the now nearly empty aorta to help restore blood pressure; I temporarily pinch this viaduct, which carries blood and oxygen to the rest of the body, closed. At the same time, I assist every other heartbeat with a compression of the heart.

The heart is nearly empty. Henry puts in a large IV in the subclavian vein on the right side just below the collarbone. Anesthesia puts in a large internal-jugular-neck IV line, and already I can feel the room warming up. Hypothermia (low temperature) causes clotting to collapse, so we want the room to be sweltering. I'm still pinching the aorta with my left hand, and with the flat part of my open right hand, I'm still assisting this kid's heart—every other beat. Suddenly my hands start to feel different. As if they are being guided, a serenade of sorts begins.

In the operating room, there is a duality of emotion. A battle develops. I imagine hearing the voice of an announcer before a boxing match. "On this side, in bloody clothes with nearly no vital signs, the patient and his trauma—violence, death, hate, awful circumstance—and on the other side in green scrubs, the trauma team with tools for survival."

Who will win?

8

Having worked with many patients and having heard stories about near death and "white-light experiences," I realize this is one of those cases. This young man is at the line of clinical death (no vital signs), and somewhere over that line is biological brain death.

For a few seconds, his heart stops, crossing the line.

The tempo quickens as I squeeze the heart between my first four fingers and thumb, with care toward not pressing too hard. New transfused blood enters his veins and rushes to the right side of the heart, then to the lungs, and back to the left side of the heart. After a brief period on the other side of the line of life, his heart starts to beat again.

I feel the heart getting fuller, but still my fingers keep the aorta pinched. The aorta is the large artery that comes off the heart and gives blood, with red blood cells carrying oxygen to the abdomen, kidneys, and legs. An artery is a blood vessel that goes away from the heart; the aorta is the largest artery in the body. Blood flows through the aorta just like water through a garden hose.

Is this a white-light moment for this young man?

In layperson literature, a white-light moment involves a person who is close to death seeing a bright light and hearing beautiful music. When I feel such a moment is happening, I try to be on my best behavior, because if a white-light experience is truly occurring—where music is playing and an opening in heaven is created—it's possible that my mom might be looking down on me. My goal is to save this kid. Will the "white-light people" be upset with me if this young man survives? Angry at having to call the whole thing off.

After this near-death patient's pressure heads back toward a life-supporting level, Janelle changes positions with me and places her hands inside the chest. She receives a brief tutorial on how to pinch the aorta, and now the actual operation can begin. The case for urgency in this trauma can be argued with a pizza analogy.

Years ago Domino's stated that if they did not deliver a pizza within thirty minutes, the customer would get the pizza for free. Well, this type of trauma is like ordering a pizza, and if you don't stop the bleeding within thirty minutes, either the patient dies, or you've created a world of hurt for yourself and the patient in the coming days and weeks. So our challenge is to stop the bleeding within thirty minutes, and ten minutes already have gone by.

The anesthesia doctor, Rick, (aka "Annie") is a veteran anesthesiologist nearing the end of his career. He has seen everything and half-wonders whether this patient will survive. He also wonders what the use is in saving a kid who may well be a gangbanger. Rick seems to have a bit of a jaundiced view of things.

He asks me, "Would you like to listen to a little reggae music?"

I nod "yes." With my scalpel I make an incision from just below the sternum directly in the middle, straight down, around the belly button, and down to the pubis.

There are different types of pubi. There is the symphysis pubis, the mons pubis, and the pubis-pubis. Like a barker at a carnival, and concealing a snicker under my mask, I ask the medical student, "Janelle, what's the pubis-pubis?"

Still concentrating on pinching the aorta and watching every heartbeat through the chest opening, she quips, "I do not know, sir, but I will find out and report back to you."

The young medical student feels good that she is being treated as an equal and feels proud of the trust that has been heaped upon her in this life-or-death drama. Hitting the jackpot, I see that Elsie is my scrub nurse. She's an older lady with gray hair and has deep lines in her African-American skin; her face tells a story. She didn't finish high school but has five kids who are all professionals. She has the skill of a concert pianist and has few equals. Elsie has experienced the roller coaster of life; one word describes her—"understanding."

Upon entering the abdomen, we are met with an ocean of blood, waves of red heme, crashing and foaming onto the floor.

"Elsie, laps!"

"Lap" stands for laparotomy sponge—a small white towel about the size of a washcloth with a little magnetic ring on it for X-ray identification purposes. There's so much blood in the belly; it must be soaked up so that the source of bleeding can be found. It looks like this young man has lost at least 80 percent of his blood. Twenty laps are placed in the right lower quadrant, twenty in the left lower quadrant, twenty in the left upper quadrant, and twenty in the right upper quadrant. That's eighty laps total, which we combine with suction. Eventually all the blood is soaked up, which allows us to see the sites of injuries.

Our attention quickly goes to the right lower quadrant area, where there is obvious injury to both the small and large intestine—two bullet holes in each. Brisk arterial and venous bleeding is coming from the right lower quadrant. After placing strategic retractors, we see that the hemorrhage from the right-lower-quadrant artery and vein is very deep in the pelvis.

Henry holds pressure in this area with ten lap sponges, which gives us a little time to consider our options. The injuries to the intestines are manageable. Bowel clamps above and below the gunshot areas are placed at each bullet hole to control the leakage of stool.

A quick check with "Annie" reveals that he and the massive transfusion nurse have given this young man eleven units of packed red blood cells and four units of fresh frozen plasma; platelets are on the way. Blood pressure is eighty over forty; heart rate is 140. We're still in big trouble.

With Henry still holding pressure in the deep pelvis, I say, "Let's take a peek."

As soon as he takes off the pressure, wicked arterial and venous bleeding occurs. It's necessary to clamp the large vessels that lead into the right lower quadrant. Mostly with touch and instinct, and not so much with my eyes, I enter the back compartment in the abdomen where the large arteries and veins run like high-flow pipelines.

After I've controlled the distal aorta and cava with clamps, I tell Janelle that she can let loose of the aorta in the chest and come on down with us in the belly. We take a little peek into the right lower quadrant again, and still there's wicked arterial and venous bleeding, only temporized by Henry's twenty laps' worth of manual pressure.

Henry places fresh laparotomy pads in the lower quadrant area, deep in the pelvis, and continues to hold pressure from above. He's just a third-year surgery resident, but he knows we're in big trouble.

Looking at me with almost completely fogged glasses and beads of sweat on his forehead, Henry wonders out loud, "Doc, what are we going to do?"

Realizing the bleeding is very difficult to control, and in my years, having seen similar patients as this die, I reply, "Well, Henry, we're going to have to do the Bagdad procedure."

He knows there's no such thing as the Baghdad procedure, but still he asks, "Doc, what's the Bagdad procedure?"

"OK, let me show you."

My incision starts in the right groin area, close to the proximal thigh, and with a knife and scissors, I take the incision right down to the femoral vein. The veins are blood vessels that take blood back up to the heart. Next I take the dissection on top of the vein in the groin to the groin ligament—the inguinal ligament—which I divide into two. Next stop is the cord structure, which is encircled and preserved. Following the femoral vein, I take a dive down into the pelvis on top of the common femoral branch to the iliac vein, dividing every bit of skin and subcutaneous tissue and muscle. This includes division of the external oblique, internal oblique, transversalis, and rectus muscles, thus dividing this young man's "six-pack." He will now have a challenge regaining his six-pack, although if he survives, it certainly won't be impossible.

I connect the groin incision with the midline abdominal incision, and upon connecting the last little bit of skin, I see that the entire area is splayed open in the most remarkable way.

"Henry, get yourself a vascular clamp. I want you to put clamps above and below the area of arterial hemorrhage."

Clamps in hand, Henry places the first one, and then, like duck soup, he places the second one.

"Great work, big guy. Now clamp above and below the venous injury."

The Baghdad procedure has provided such good exposure that Henry, who's not even a fully trained surgeon, is able to put the clamps in place. He looks at me and I look at him; twenty-seven minutes have passed since this young man arrived. We've stopped the bleeding, and the pizza hasn't even arrived yet. Whoo-ah! We use a 5-0 Prolene suture and a 4-0 Prolene suture to repair the damaged artery and vein. Vascular clamps are removed, circulation is restored, hemostasis—control of bleeding—is documented. Next we'll do a two-layer repair of the injured bowel, and we'll be good.

"Henry, go ahead and close up the thoracotomy (chest incision) and put in two chest tubes. Janelle and I will get his belly closed."

The patient has stabilized. Even Bob Marley appears to be singing a little bit stronger. We all laugh as "Red Red Wine" starts to play, since the whole floor and OR table are soaked with blood—red, red wine indeed! As we finish closing the chest and belly and apply the dressings, I ask the OR nurses if one of them will call report to the ICU.

CHAPTER 2

⚭

Elsie called report to Nurse Betsy in the ICU. The first thing Betsy asked was "Who's the trauma surgeon?"

Upon hearing it was Dr. Chollet, Betsy felt at ease because she knew his patients somehow did better, probably because he always tried to stop the bleeding within thirty minutes. He was known as somewhat of an old-school trauma surgeon despite only being thirty-two years old. Per his CV the nurses knew he was East Coast–trained and had specialty training in vascular surgery. Betsy remembered going out with Hillary and Henry and some of the nurses for a few drinks one night. She remembered hearing Hillary talk about his mentor, Dr. Frederick Reichle, and how much he had learned from him. Along with the correct way to do things, he also witnessed some incorrect ways. Betsy was struck by Hillary's extreme dedication to medicine and knew it would be tough for any woman to compete with this doctor's number-one love—being a surgeon.

It typically took the anesthesia doctor and OR nurses five to ten minutes to get all of the lines and IVs straight, and to switch the patient to a portable heart monitor. During this time, Hillary, Henry, and Janelle changed their bloody booties and put on fresh, clean ones. Because the room was so warm, all three were sweating—Hillary like a pig, and Janelle and Henry like little piglets.

Janelle wrote the post-op orders as anesthesia prepared to move the patient. Hillary, Henry, and Janelle then exited the OR with an anesthesiologist, a respiratory therapist, and an anesthesia resident. Patient and monitors all ready, they made a sharp left turn and came to a pair of sliding glass doors that "Annie" unlocked with a swipe of his ID badge. This trauma center had three ICUs, and the patient was assigned to room 1101 in ICU A. Hospital security was guarding the ICU waiting room, and because this was a shooting, two LAPD officers also were present. Inside the waiting room, at least twenty-five people were waiting to hear from the trauma surgeon. Hillary told Henry, "Go ahead and get the patient situated and write the rest of the orders. Janelle and I will talk with the family."

The security guard asked, "Doc, you want me to put them in the quiet room?"

Hillary felt it wouldn't be necessary because everything basically had gone smoothly, and most likely this patient would survive.

Then the LAPD officer asked, "Doc, can I talk to you for a second?"

Hillary knew exactly what the officer was going to say. A hundred times in a row they had asked him how he spelled his name, and then they asked him whether the patient would survive.

Hillary answered, "Sure, Officer."

The officer reached into his left shirt pocket, pulled out a pad and a pen, opened the pad to the first page, and asked, "Doc, how do you spell your name?"

Hillary looked directly at his ID badge and replied, "C-h-o-l-l-e-t."

"OK, Doc. Thanks. Now I have another question."

The question that was always asked came out. "Doc, is he going to make it?"

"I can't say for sure, but things look pretty good. I give him a ninety-percent chance of pulling through, even though on paper it's only fifty-fifty."

"OK. Thanks, Doc," the officer said. As he and his partner walked away, he called his sergeant and relayed the information. Both officers breathed sighs of relief because the homicide team wouldn't have to be called, which meant far less paperwork.

Finished with police business at least for now, Hillary turned his attention to the family. Both Hillary and Janelle were glad that their young patient had survived, because occasionally when a patient didn't survive, depending on the circumstance, the family and friends flipped out.

Hillary remembered one time when one of the ER docs went into the waiting room. She was actually a trauma surgeon who somehow lost the desire to do trauma surgery and went back and did a four-year ER residency to become an ER doc. After she told a family that their relative had died, one of the men punched her in the face and knocked her unconscious.

In this case, there was relatively good news that the young man probably would survive despite his severe injuries. Hillary and Janelle went to the front of the waiting room and positioned themselves at the arch of the entrance, and then asked to speak with the family of Roberto. When all twenty-five stepped forward, Hillary said, "Whoa, hold on. I want to talk to two people who are the spokespeople. Are there a mom and dad? Everyone else can listen."

A man and a woman stepped forward. Both were Hispanic and only the woman understood and spoke English. "I am Roberto's mom," she said. "And this is his dad, Roberto Senior."

Thinking that the two parents couldn't be much older than thirty, Hillary said, "I'm Dr. Chollet. This is Janelle, my medical student. We just finished surgery on Roberto, and to start off with, I'd like to say that he's stable and he's alive. I want to add that this is basically a miracle because he came in with his heart barely beating, and at one point his heart stopped. He was shot in the belly, and we were able to repair his injuries."

Knowing that to a family this could be confusing, Hillary drew a picture on a blank piece of paper on his clipboard, described the injuries, and drew a diagram of everything they had done in surgery. Next he drew a graph that showed the trimodal pattern of mortality in trauma. Basically this described the three times after trauma when people most often died. He showed the family that the first hump was at six hours and said that of all the people who do not make it, that was when a good many of them die. The second hump was from twenty-four to thirty-six hours; the third was from days to weeks later. The third hump was made up of complications from blood clots and infection. It seemed that the family understood his explanations, but Hillary didn't expect them to remember everything, especially because of the magnitude of the trauma.

He further explained that Roberto's on-paper odds were fifty-fifty but added that, in his own experience; he had lost only about 1.7 percent of his trauma patients who had made it to the emergency room with a heartbeat.

"I'm going to treat Roberto as if he were my son or my brother," he told the mother.

The family was very happy, but in a somewhat sheepish manner, they seemed to want to hear one more thing. When they asked, "What can we do?" Hillary said, "You can do what I'm going to do right now, and that is to say a prayer to the good Lord."

That sealed the deal for the family; knowing that Hillary was a person of faith, they felt satisfied. A few minutes later, Henry finished writing the orders, and the three of them decided to get a bite to eat.

Janelle said, "It's five in the morning, guys."

"Janelle, it's a tradition," Henry said.

"There's only one place open at this time of night," Hillary said. "The Greasy Spoon Burrito and Taco Bar Restaurant and Lounge across the street."

It was nice and warm outside despite it being five in the morning, so the three surgeons headed to the restaurant. Janelle grabbed a table and some napkins. Henry ordered the King Kong

Burrito; Janelle ordered a fish taco and water; and Hillary ordered the Mega Mega Mega Cayente Burrito and two taquitos. In a few minutes their orders were ready, and the trio sat down and started on their early-morning feast. Both Henry and Hillary squirted on extra hot sauce. Hillary felt a bit of regret for adding the extra hot sauce and looked over at Henry's burrito. It was (no lie) at least a foot long. Being much younger, this third-year surgery resident was better able to tolerate the extreme amount of heat and spice without developing reflux and the acidic feeling of having a volcano in his chest.

After three or four bites, each of the surgeons felt much better. Henry asked, "Doc, what's the Baghdad procedure?"

Hillary thought for a moment and then said, "Honestly, dude, we were in such trouble that somehow I just thought it up. I didn't want to let the kid die and at the same time decided to call it the Baghdad procedure so a certain alpha-male trauma surgeon—namely Dr. Puler—wouldn't know where it came from."

Janelle seemed interested in the idea of being so close to death and asked Hillary what it felt like to save someone.

"To tell you the truth, Janelle," he said, "it feels good. The feeling of saving someone is a soft feeling of satisfaction in your heart, but the feeling of losing someone, especially if the patient slips through your fingers, hits you in your gut. It's a stressful deal, balancing life and death and having one's being in your hands. It's like holding an expensive crystal vase—and it comes with the possibility of my making a mistake and accidentally fumbling, juggling, and dropping the expensive crystal, hearing it crash, and then seeing it shatter on the ground to the horror of everyone watching. Yes, watching the patient crash and burn and die because of *me*!"

Janelle partly understood. Henry understood more. Hillary remembered a poem he had first read years ago. "Guys, here's a poem my dad sent me when I was in medical school," he said. "It's titled, 'You.'

> "Your fund of knowledge increases as a medical student and drops off once you become an intern.
> You think you know a lot by the time you finish your internship.
> You start your residency being afraid and not knowing enough.
> By the time you are a chief resident, you feel pretty confident.
> By the time you finish your chief residency, you think you have
> a lot to learn.
> When you do a fellowship, you think you don't know much at the outset.
> By the time you finish, you think you know a little bit more, and as the years go by, you feel more and more confident, more and more learned, and then you die."

Henry and Janelle looked at each other then back at Hillary. Then Janelle said, "Die? I'm sure there's some message in that poem, but I still have two hundred and fifty thousand dollars in school loans. No time to die for this chick."

Henry couldn't stop laughing, and Hillary thought the meaning was lost with how he had recited the poem. Maybe it was a generational thing.

As Janelle, Henry, and Hillary were finishing their fiesta, the events of the day caught up with Janelle, and she asked Hillary, "How do you cope with all of the craziness of your job? What helps you in your thought process? So far we haven't learned this in medical school."

Henry, who had been subjected to three years of extreme craziness, wanted to hear the answer as well.

The senior doc said, "Well, imagine the game Dungeons & Dragons."

The two younger docs looked at each other and could hardly believe their boss was talking about Dungeons & Dragons. Also known as D&D, the game was developed in 1974. Since then it had undergone multiple modifications, but basically it was a fantasy game of conflict mostly played by college students.

The bleary-eyed trauma surgeon said, "Medicine is like Dungeons & Dragons, but this version is real, not imaginary or fantasy. There are rules of engagement, but it's important to realize that as a surgeon you have only one life. At all costs, you must protect your life. Guys, look at it as if medicine is one big game. It's a high-stakes game, for sure. Remember that you must protect your own life, and also remember that with any game; ultimately it's more satisfying if you play fairly. Forget for a moment what all the philosophers have to say, and go back to the Golden Rule. It may well be 'He, who has the gold makes the rules,' but, as we all learned in kindergarten, the Golden Rule says, 'Do unto others as you would have them do unto you.' When playing this game, one must realize that there is etiquette and that it's important to maintain one's cool and also keep one's dignity.

"Imagine you have the cool of James Bond and the wisdom of Ben Franklin. There are those who play unfairly and are cheaters. Play fairly, and the fruits of winning will be all the sweeter. The game of medicine is definitely harder these days. Some of the supplemental rules of this game can be drawn from past literature. Remember George Orwell and *Animal Farm*? 'All animals are created equal, but some are more equal than others.' This is a very important rule that primarily comes into play with hospital administrators. The way they treat certain doctors—well, the administrators' approach generally is to set up a directorship, pay them money, and then when it's time to make a decision in their favor, the administrators call in their chips and the doctors vote the way the administrators want. In exchange, by selling themselves out, the doctors curry favor and become some of the 'more equal animals.' We da hoes. Dey da pimps. Other books administrators read are *The Art of War* by Sun Tzu, *The Communist Manifesto*, and Mao's *The Little Red Book*."

Janelle and Henry looked at each other and half-wondered whether their boss was a little wacky, but as they thought about it, within the context of a game, it sounded about right. The two junior docs mused that Dungeons & Dragons and Medicine—The Game sounded like a fun game, albeit a high-stakes one.

Henry asked, "How do you get an edge by playing fairly?"

"I'll teach you two ways to get an edge," Hillary said. "The first is through the Socratic Method, and the second is through something I'll teach you in the next few weeks. It's called 'quiet eyes.' "

With that tutorial, the medical student and the third-year resident felt the whole night had been worthwhile. But Hillary himself, although a spiritual person, hadn't quite reconciled the moral overlap between this D&D game of medicine and his theological beliefs. Although he was raised Catholic, he felt that the traditional rules made up by the Catholic Church were ones that were seemingly bent into many convenient forms by the *Animal Farm* theologians, administrators, and businesspeople, especially lawyers. He also felt he was on a proper moral plane and that his Catholic "perspective" was something he would need to further examine and ultimately reconcile. After a few last tortilla chips with guacamole and hot sauce, the trio had a lot on their minds and more work to do.

They'd poured out their emotions to one another, and their understanding had reached new levels, as had their incurable indigestion. The weary three finished up and walked outside. The sun was starting to rise; it was almost 6:30 a.m., and Hillary would be off trauma call in a half hour. He said, "Guys, I'm going to go back to the call room for a few minutes, see my patients in the hospital, and then go home to sleep. Thanks for tonight. You're the greatest."

Henry and Janelle headed back into the hospital. Even though they barely had slept a wink all night, they were ready to start their day's work.

CHAPTER 3

❧

After rounds Hillary walked to his car with the goal of going home and to sleep. As he entered the doctors' parking lot, his thoughts went to his car and where he had parked. Not able to recall because he had been awake for forty-eight hours, he pressed his Volvo key twice.

Chirp, chirp.

"Ah, just a few rows away."

So tired he was barely able to focus, he slid into the driver's seat and remembered that his seat could be adjusted seventy-eight ways. He tilted it back, then up, then down, then...*snore, snore, snore...* He was sound asleep.

Fifteen minutes later his beeper went off.

It was the ICU with post-op labs on Roberto. Hillary made a few vent changes and gave an order for 3:00 p.m. labs. He almost felt too tired to sleep. With his eyes closed, in between awake and asleep, he thought about his dad's birthday in two days. He was so tired he was experiencing a "flight of ideas" and tangential reasoning; memories flooded both his conscious and unconscious. The rising sun shone through the front window of his fourteen-year-old car and jolted him awake.

He spoke out loud to himself. "It's time to go home and lie down in my comfy bed." He started his car but couldn't remember where he lived. Having experienced this situation before, he reached for his GPS navigation and touched the avatar "Home."

Slick trick, he thought, as the nice lady said, "Turn left now, and turn right in two miles."

The tired doc thought she sounded pretty smart, probably knew physics, and from the sound of her voice, had nice feet and beautiful toes with French nails. So tired that he was falling in love with the GPS lady, Hillary finally made it to his little apartment.

"Ah, home at last."

Up fifteen stairs, then a twist of the key, and he was inside. Bed in sight, still in scrubs, he kicked off his shoes and fell onto his bed and dozed off.

He was still asleep some eight hours later when his cell phone rang. It was Maureen.

"Hi, Mo."

"Hi, baby," she responded. "You must be exhausted."

Hillary disregarded his fatigue and said, "Come over for dinner."

Mo had known her "baby" for only three months but had full trust in him. "Sure," she said. "How about some Thai?"

"Mmm…that sounds great. You choose. I'll open a bottle of wine."

Forty minutes later Mo let herself in with her key. Thai food in tow, she kissed her man and started to set up for dinner. Lettuce wraps, spicy fish soup, Thai barbecue ribs, rice, and veggies, along with wine, made for a nice evening.

After dinner the couple took their glasses of pinot grigio and sat side by side on the couch in front of the wood-burning fireplace. Mo felt she was falling in love and wanted to know more about Hillary. She had met his dad two months ago but didn't have an understanding of his past since he couldn't talk. "Hill, tell me about your mom and dad."

The more reserved Hillary figured he should tell his story so that Mo could grasp what she was getting herself into.

"Well, baby," he said, "let me start from the beginning. This is a long story, but I owe it to you, so settle in."

Mo took a sip of wine. "I'm ready."

Still sitting, Hill began, "Having a great mom and dad gives a kid a big boost in life. Of course circumstances are never perfect, and all families have their problems and issues. Dad was a person who was bigger than my surrounding world. He also was smart, strong, and a helper of people and animals alike. My first dog was a little fox terrier named Tiny. The bond between a boy and his dog is like no other. One day Tiny woke up with a big, painful bulge in her groin. Dad diagnosed an incarcerated hernia and asked me to hold my suffering little dog while he went to his office. A short time later, we went to the changing room near our swimming pool. Dad, our gardener Mr. Armijo, and I operated on Tiny and fixed her hernia. At seven years of age, I was impressed with how Dad had saved Tiny.

"Dad was my instant hero, and from that day on, I wanted to be a doctor just like him. The next day my canine pal was up and about, eating and drinking, and I remember Dad saying that everything was going to be fine.

"Over the years it felt like he was a modern-day legend. Growing up in New Orleans, he was the youngest of three. Olga, his mom—my grandma—was Cajun. Deserted by my grandfather, she survived by scrubbing floors. Exactly how Dad grew up isn't clear. One thing is clear, though. The Canal Street parish system collectively helped raise him and his two brothers. It was said the family was so poor that when invited to play football with the big kids, my dad got his sneakers from the next-door neighbor's trash. Eventually, both he and his brothers showed their prowess in football, basketball, baseball, and track.

"At Holy Cross High School, the Chollets won city and state championships in football and basketball. At one point my dad and his two brothers were three of the starting five on the basketball team. Besides being good in basketball and excellent in football, Dad was a scholar to boot.

"Perhaps wise beyond his years, he was very serious in his studies and wanted to be a doctor. His last year in high school went by pretty fast, as he was heavily recruited by colleges and universities across the country: Notre Dame, Ohio State, Cornell, Tulane, LSU, and others.

"LSU and Tulane were the local schools and the aspiration of a lot of young men in the region. Because my dad's mom was starting to get a little bit older, and because she had been worn down by the years of sacrifice, he decided to go to Tulane. However, he didn't go. He was accepted, but then one day he was notified that they had rescinded his acceptance.

"Some forty-five years later, after researching our family heritage, we found out that around the turn of the century an African American woman entered our family. This woman, whose name was Olivia Olinde, was the daughter of a slave. Her son was my father's father. My dad was one-eighth African and seven-eighths white. When Tulane found out he had 'black blood' in him, they quietly withdrew his acceptance.

"Things worked out for him nonetheless. With the guidance of his church and coach, he decided to go to college at Cornell University in Ithaca, New York. At Cornell he became an all-American in football. He played on the varsity football and basketball teams for four years and was voted Cornell's best scholar-athlete.

"After finishing his college career in sports, he was drafted by the Cleveland Rams professional football team and was also offered a position on the Syracuse Nationals—a professional basketball team. In addition, he received an offer to attend medical school at McGill University and to play football in the Canadian Football League. After talking with his coach, he decided to go to Cornell medical school.

"Reading the tea leaves of his past, one sees a spiritual thread in the fabric of his persona that guided his decisions. It almost seemed predestined. Some people, however, thought my dad was from the wrong side of the tracks, especially when he met a beautiful coed also attending Cornell. Janet was a very fair-skinned, slim, beautiful, smart lady whose mother was a college professor and whose father was a scientist. Now enter Hillary—'dark skinned' and from N'awlins. Taking after her mother, Janet had a mind of her own and years later confessed, "I fell in love because he was shy and kind, and he had an eye toward helping people." The couple fell in love and got married in 1955. Claiming my dad was too 'Cajun looking' for his Scottish liking, her father refused to go to the wedding!

"Mo, once again, I have to say how blessed I've been to have a great mom and dad. I was afforded very special opportunities. When I was a freshman in college, Mom passed away. It isn't clear exactly what happened, but it appears it was an accidental overdose of sleeping medicine. I was away at college and asleep on the couch in my apartment. Around four in the morning I was awakened with a chill going through my body. A few minutes later my brother Jon called and said, 'Mom's dead, can you come home?' This crushed all of us. Dad always had helped people, but he wasn't able to save the one closest to him.

"Losing mom so suddenly and not being able to say good-bye deeply affected me. She was everything to me. I think that's why I went into trauma to help give patients and families an official 'second chance when faced with potential loss.' "

Mo looked into Hill's eyes and could see the heartache and his soft vulnerable side.

"After my mom passed away, Dad fell apart. He was permanently scarred. Several years later, his mom, Olga, came down with esophageal cancer and moved to California to live with us. At that time I was away at college, soon to start medical school. Being lonely, Dad craved companionship and took up with a woman who was much, much younger than him.

"Olga, was definitely a truth teller and feisty, even with cancer and osteoporosis. This bent-over old Cajun woman could still call a spade a spade, saying to this woman, 'Yo ar nothing but a ho, a common ho. Yo do not have a pot to piss in, no a window to thro it out.' Olga was a truth seeker."

Maureen laughed and at the same time wiped a tear from her eye.

"She told me that my father, Hillary, Sr., was named after Saint Hilary, who, back in the year three hundred AD, was born a pagan into a family of nobility. In college I did some research on Saint Hilary. After receiving teachings in Greek on Neo-Platonism, which included learning about mystical philosophy based on Plato, Saint Hilary studied the Old and New Testaments and converted to Christianity. As a person of faith, he was later baptized.

"After Olga passed away, while I was in medical school, my dad came down with Lou Gehrig's disease. This is a devastating illness. It has a sporadic—or mixed-genetic—expression, and unfortunately it also infected my dad's brother and one of our cousins.

31

This muscle-paralyzing illness affects the motor or muscle parts of the body while one's mind stays completely intact.

"Over the years Dad developed weak arms, and his speech became garbled. His surgical partner thought he was coming to the hospital drunk. After a trip to Scripps Institute in San Diego, the diagnosis was certain.

"Being a doctor, Dad thought he had picked up a virus in the fertilizer from some football turf. One doctor at Scripps thought his condition was somehow related to the polio virus because Dad had worked with kids on the polio ward both in college and medical school.

"Soon he started to drool and had to walk around the house with a washcloth in his mouth, soaking up the drool. At that time he was still able to move his arms. One day I came home from medical school for a visit. My brother Jon and I were talking to Dad, who was always very competitive. He said he wanted to play a game of HORSE.

"HORSE is a basketball game where the first person shoots from any place on the court. If the shot is made, and if the other people playing can't make the exact same shot, they all get an 'H.' The next shot they miss, they get an 'O,' then an 'R,' then an 'S,' and finally an 'E.' After you get 'HORSE,' you're out.

"Dad, who was really starting to suffer from Lou Gehrig's disease, was still able to bend his arms but no longer able to practice surgery, which he loved so much. He actually beat my brother and me in a game of HORSE. Imagine that! After the game, as we were walking past our tennis court, Dad decided he wanted to jump over the net. Handing us his drool-catching washcloth, perhaps for a moment imagining himself back to his old self, he took six quick steps—for a moment we thought he was going to make it—and boom! He caught his toe on the net and landed face first. My brother and I were half-terrified and half-laughing at the same time. Dad was laughing and crying too. I felt like his tears were an expression of pent-up emotion and an honorable admission that he was no longer the one that helped but the one who needed help. And just like when we were little kids and fell, and Dad would help us up and dust us off, my brother and I raced to help him. Before we knew it, all three of us were laughing and crying. Soon after that, Dad could no longer eat. Fighting the battle of his life, he decided to get a feeding tube, and after the feeding tube was in, he'd put his food in a blender and then squirt it down his own tube, trying to keep himself strong. But he was having more and more trouble with breathing and clearing his secretions—sputum and drool.

"My sister was just starting medical school, and I was finishing my surgery residency. Dad really wanted to see us finish, so he got a tracheostomy. Several months later he went on a respirator."

Hillary looked at Mo and shrugged, moved his head from side to side, and lamented over his dad's illness. He then looked down, saddened, and said, "And now his birthday is coming up. Worlds of emotion and events have happened. Now he's only able to blink his eyes and cry. What a trooper. I don't completely understand what keeps him going, but as I look back, I have knowledge of the strength with which he has lived his life, and I also have an understanding of his weaknesses.

"He wasn't a political person and didn't like to fight the battles of competition despite being an athlete. Dad believed that your natural talents and intellect and ability should stand for themselves. As I reflect on the important things I know about his life, I'm still slightly mystified by him. To me, he's definitively bigger than life."

Mo wiped a tear from her cheek and threw herself toward Hillary, who wrapped his arms around her thin frame and gave her a soft kiss on the lips. "I'm falling in love with you," he told her.

Mo squealed and then quietly responded, "Me too. Thanks for telling me your story. It was beautiful."

Seeing the late hour—11:00 p.m.—the couple kissed each other good night, and Hillary walked Mo to her car. Another kiss good night and she headed home.

Hillary headed back upstairs and reviewed the night's events. He was ready for bed and figured Mo had made it home. He sent her a text that read, "U me kiss hold hug tongue love nitey nite xoxoxoxoxo."

CHAPTER 4

᠁

T he morning sun had risen, and as the dew started to evaporate off the leaves in his expansive garden, Hillary, Sr., sat in his wheelchair and enjoyed the majestic view before him. Not able to breathe in the rose-scented air from the garden, his lungs were filled twelve times per minute with oxygen from a tank strapped to his wheelchair and delivered through an air hose hooked to a tube in his trachea that entered through a hole in his throat. Tied into his wheelchair for protection, and slightly leaning backward to prevent a free fall to the ground, the doc heard the buzzing of a hummingbird behind him, and then in an instant the bird was before him. He saw the dancing bird flutter from flower to flower and was glad he still had at least two of his five senses.

Unable to move any of the muscles in his body, he could only blink his eyes and cry. His face appeared to display a single emotion—a frozen mask of what appeared to be horror—but the expression was merely the result of paralyzed facial muscles. He was now five years into his Lou Gehrig's disease adventure.

He welcomed this day as a wonderful one, since it represented an additional day that he was alive and able to enjoy life and his family. He had two sons and one daughter. Jon was in business, and Hillary, Jr., his older son, was also a surgeon. His daughter Janet, the baby of the family, was an OB/GYN doctor.

As Hillary enjoyed the early-morning hour, he noted that he had some irritation in his tracheostomy. Since he had a portable, battery-powered breathing machine, there was no cord or tether. So, for at least a few hours, he was free. He considered the day before him; today was his birthday. The stricken surgeon was thankful he could still think and reminisce about his past.

His mind wandered back to one night when he and Hillary and Janet were having dinner at home. As he fed himself through his feeding tube, he had said, "When I get worse, when I can no longer talk and say what's bothering me, please make sure I don't sit on my balls. You have to promise me that whenever you see me, or whoever is taking care of me, you'll make sure my balls and scrotum are elevated. If need be, put a washcloth underneath them."

The memory made him laugh on the inside since he could no longer laugh on the outside.

He heard Maya approach. Her voice and face were a welcome sight. Maya was a fiftyish woman with a Creole accent who suddenly had showed up several years ago. She was a registered nurse and originally from New Orleans. Almost immediately Hillary took a liking to her. Maya was dark skinned, neatly coiffed, and dressed in a nurse's outfit with a colorful apron.

"Good morning, Doctor," she said. "It's another wonderful day. Praise Jesus that we have yet another day to celebrate. Oh, and happy birthday! Tonight we're having a birthday party for you in honor of your sixty-third birthday. This will be a long day for you, but everyone is looking forward to seeing you."

Hillary reflected on his past birthdays and the high and low points of his life. As a doctor, he realized his existence had been between the lines of tragedy and survival. On the one hand, he was happy to have another birthday, but on the other, he felt like a prisoner in his own body. He wished he could continue to contribute in some way.

Maya and Hillary shared a special connection. She reached into her pocket and took out a gold coin a little bigger than a silver dollar and put it in Hillary's outstretched hand, his fingers stiff. Maya wrapped his fingers around the coin. Her simple touch felt good, and the personal meaning of the gold object reminded him of his years of service and faith-filled past. As he couldn't move his fingers even a little, this tiny movement gave him the same joy felt by a wanderer in the Sahara Desert who sees a mirage but finds water after all.

The doc imagined he was that man in the desert and was once again able to run and use his arms and legs. He relished the sensation of freedom from paralysis, as fountains of cool water flowed over his head, face, and body. The sentiment and special meaning of the moment were made evident by Hillary's only outward way of communicating, as several tears flowed from his eyes. Maya saw the tears, took her hankie, and wiped under his eyes. Glad she had a supply of hankies for her boss and friend, she said, "Doc, let's go inside. We have lots to do before the party."

Maya turned the wheelchair away from the morning sun and headed up the walkway to the house. With pleasure she remembered back to when he could still write and how he once called her his angel.

Hillary looked at the house and reflected back over the years. He was thankful he had a nice place to live. Over the years, before she passed away, his wife, Janet, had been able (through careful finance management) to buy more than fifty pieces of real estate and turn their family situation into one of prosperity. Now Hillary was blessed to live on a two-acre estate with a long winding driveway in Bel Air, California.

Hillary lived in his large house with round-the-clock nursing and respiratory therapy. Maya was the head nurse, but she seemed to have a spiritual mission as well. As Maya and Hillary entered the house, Pascal, the family Saint Bernard, greeted them. He was eight years old and friendly to all; the pooch's single fault was that he was a drooler. Maya hooked the doc back up to his A/C power outlet and tuned his MP3 player to a medley of James Taylor. Pascal laid his head on Hillary's lap in an attempt to soothe and guard his master.

CHAPTER 5

⟨∞⟩

I t was 5:15 p.m., and as Mo got dressed, she thought about tonight's birthday party. Usually somewhat restrained, she didn't
mind this time how she felt. Dizzy feelings and a stomach full of butterflies had flooded her heart and told her she was madly in love.

With long blonde hair and a slim figure, the thirty-two-year-
old woman, who was an actress, slipped into her stockings, then
her form-fitting slightly-above-the-knee-length dress, and three-
and-a-half-inch high heels. A few spritzes of Chanel No. 5, and
she was ready.

Maureen picked up her diary and reread her July 24 entry:

My man:

*Hillary's sun-kissed skin glows with the blush of a sensitive
schoolboy, especially when given a compliment.*

He has a demure shyness—oftentimes seen as a quiet transparency in his soft velvet-brown eyes. A sparkle of tenderness radiates as they shift away at the onset of attention upon him.

Beautiful, wavy locks of shimmery black hair, with just a few silver-stroked strands etching along his hairline next to his ears, give a mark of distinction and character to his already handsome looks.

Soft and tender lips form a balanced shape with a slightly fuller lower lip—irresistible to kiss! An athletic build both lean and toned, his five foot eleven frame makes a perfect dreamboat of a man for me.

More than his masculine, rugged exterior of flesh and bones is the inner vortex of his treasure-filled heart of pure gold. I am drawn to his kindness, intelligence, and deep perceptive abilities.

I believe him to be loyal. He is wonderful—my best friend and true love. Oh, and his witty dry sense of humor.

To sum it up, I would have to say Hillary is perfect for me.

—Maureen

Mo tried to stay grounded as she picked up her smartphone and pressed "Hillary."

After eight rings, he picked up. "Hello, Hill," she said. "Are you ready?"

Hillary, who had been roused from a deep sleep, used only twenty-five of his one hundred-plus IQ points. He grunted, "Hello."

Mo, who was generally very prompt, responded, "In a half hour we have to be at your dad's house. It's his birthday."

Hillary groaned, "Oh, man! OK, OK."

The beautiful woman felt for Hillary and what he had been through. She felt for his agonizing, tired, worn-down state, which prompted her to say, "Honey, I'll be over in fifteen minutes to pick you up."

"Thanks sweetie, I'll be ready. Bye."

Mo locked up and jumped into her nearly ten-year-old, two-door Mercedes convertible and drove toward Hillary's apartment. She listened to classical music—J.S. Bach—and the fifteen-minute drive passed quickly.

After carefully parking her "little baby," she hustled up the cobblestone path toward Hillary's apartment, which wasn't in a very nice or safe area. *What's with Hill?* she wondered. His family seemed well off, and he was a young trauma and vascular surgeon making good money, but he appeared to hold on to an old way of doing things.

Up the fifteen steps to Hill's apartment, Mo felt no pain in her calves since she worked out every day. Briefly she thought back to earlier in the day when she was auditioning for a role in a TV series as a lawyer—what a difference between lawyers and doctors!

She reached into her purse and found her key, slid it into the deadbolt lock, twisted the key, gave two quick knocks, and entered the apartment.

"Honey, I'm here."

Hillary, who was wearing a Hawaiian shirt, blue jeans, and deck shoes, donned his dark-blue sports coat. He was unshaven and still partially asleep, but once he saw Mo and how nice she looked and smelled, he became awake and wide-eyed.

Mo grabbed his hand, headed toward the door, and said, "Let's go."

Hillary spun her around and said, "Thanks, sweetie. You're the greatest," and gave her a kiss on the lips.

Mo said, "I'd better drive."

They got into the Mercedes and drove the fifteen minutes to the birthday boy's house. The transition from Hillary's neighborhood to the Bel Air estate was gradual. When they reached the gated community, the security guard recognized Hillary and let them in. As they drove up a winding road lined by eucalyptus trees, they inhaled the wonderful smell. When they arrived at the expansive estate, they pulled into the driveway and up to a keypad and entered "1865#." Two large wrought iron gates opened inward. The winding driveway was lined with beautiful tall pine trees that transitioned into a somewhat unconventional Bohemian-style garden with stone paths and a large central veggie garden. On the right were both a swimming pool and a tennis court. Close to the house were beautiful white, yellow, and red rose bushes that lined the paths and walkways. They drove into a circular entry where there already were lots of cars. A young uniformed man directed them to pull up and told Mo he would park her car.

Hand in hand, Hillary and Mo walked toward the house. Hillary was almost six feet tall, and Mo was statuesque at five foot seven. The parking attendant took note of her blonde hair, blue eyes, and striking beauty. Mo was carrying the birthday card and present.

They rang the doorbell, and Maya opened the door and greeted them. "Hi, Doc. Hi, Miss Maureen," she said and then hugged Mo. "Sweetie, you look beautiful. Has he asked you to marry him yet? Welcome to the party."

Maya headed to the kitchen and didn't wait for the answer to her question, as she was the maestro of this party and had things to do. Once inside, the couple could see this was a Cajun-themed birthday, a Bourbon Street celebration. Green, purple, and gold lanterns decorated the spectacular circular foyer with its balcony and twenty-foot ceiling.

Green represented justice; purple, faith; and gold, power. Streamers and balloons lined the stairs that led to the balcony. Off to the right was a small bar area with a man in a tuxedo handing out drinks—champagne, along with some New Orleans classics: hurricanes and Sazerac cocktails. For the kids there were Roy Rogers and Shirley Temples. Mo took a glass of champagne, and Hillary, who wasn't on call, asked for a hurricane. Drinks in hand, the couple strolled past a formal dining room and took two steps down to a huge living room. In the corner a three-man band played fiddle, piano, and steel guitar. The trio, also in tuxedoes, played Cajun swing music from the 1940s along with a pastiche of classical tunes. Still hand in hand, the couple walked into the living room where they found lots of people mingling, including surgical and OR nurses from the hospital. All were naturally very saddened when Hillary, Sr., was diagnosed with Lou Gehrig's disease. Tonight, however, everyone was having a good time, chatting, sipping drinks, and listening to the music.

Hillary whispered into Mo's ear, "Let's go find my dad."

Hillary, Sr., was in the backyard in his wheelchair, all by himself, staring at the sunset just as the sun set over the horizon and darkness descended.

Hillary said, "Hi, Dad, happy birthday."

The senior Hillary blinked his eyes, and a tear came out.

Mo grabbed the older man's hand and gave him a kiss on his cheek. "It's getting cold out here," she said. "Let's go inside and enjoy your birthday party."

They turned around the wheelchair, which was attached to a portable respirator, and went into the living room, where a special area had been set up for Hillary, Sr. He still loved to watch basketball and football, so he had a media center and big-screen TV. Attached to his wheelchair was a gooseneck apparatus, and at the end, a small video screen along with a retinal scanner. This allowed Hillary to communicate with his eyes by focusing on words and letters and creating sentences that were translated into a voice. The young surgeon hooked his dad up but could see in his eyes that this wasn't something he was embracing. He didn't even seem interested. The young doctor, who already had seen so many patients in his career, was able to walk a mile in his father's shoes and understood how he felt. Within a minute or so, friends, colleagues, and family surrounded the elder Hillary.

Hillary, Jr., took Mo's hand. "Sweetie," he said, "I want to show you my dad's library. It's one of his favorite places."

The library was in a large circular room with beautiful mahogany floor-to-ceiling bookshelves lining the entire perimeter. The expansive room was sixteen feet tall. On the ceiling was a large fresco of *The Last Supper*. On the right side of the room, there was a row of pictures that told a story. Framed clippings from old newspapers revealed how the once-young man had played both football and basketball at Cornell University.

Hillary, Sr., had been a hero at Cornell and received the Best Athlete in the Last Fifty Years Award. A little farther down were rows and rows of medical books that dated back many years. Beautiful oil paintings, and even a drawing by Picasso, decorated the room. Toward the center of the room stood a big wooden desk, with everything on it neatly organized. A multicolored Tiffany lamp provided illumination, and underneath the lamp's light was a photograph of a young black girl, perhaps no more than eight or nine years old. This was a very old photo from before 1900. The girl wasn't wearing shoes, and she wore a tattered dress. Mo asked Hillary who the little girl was.

"Sweetie, that little girl was my great grandmother," he told her, "my dad's grandma. Olivia Olinde was her name, and her mama, Rosa, was a slave. They all lived in the Ninth Ward in New Orleans. That makes my dad one-eighth African and seven-eighths Swiss-French. That makes me one-sixteenth African and fifteen-sixteenths everything else."

Mo wiped a tear from her eye and said, "I feel an energy in this room that I've never felt before. Looking first at the power of *The Last Supper* fresco, then at this innocent little girl whose mother was a slave, I feel an ancient aura surrounding her."

As Mo contemplated, she noted the poignant distinction between the duality of suffering and survival, and felt a mixture of
emotions. She took Hillary's hand and asked, "How do you feel
about your heritage?"

"Well, sweetie, my dad grew up as a poor child without a father. He was basically raised by the church and with a history
of slavery in the family. Throughout my childhood, there was a
recurring theme of protecting the underdog. Dad instilled a confidence that you could survive and thrive but not through the
abuse of power. Throughout my life, he showed me there's more
to life than just making money; there's also the idea of service
and of helping people.

"He was a spectacular surgeon. I remember about three years
ago, when I had just started my private practice, I was doing a
Whipple. The Whipple is a surgical tour de force for a general
surgeon. It involves surgery on the pancreas and requires a great
amount of skill. The doc who was assisting me was near the end of
his career and had assisted my dad many times. After about two-and-
a-half hours, I was pretty proud of the progress we were making.

"Our operation was going along at a good pace when Dr. Ben
Bonacio, my assistant, looked up and asked, 'Are we almost done?'
Ben knew which stage of the operation we were in and how much
longer it would take, but he was relishing the opportunity to poke
fun at me and to remind me that he had helped my dad on many,
many Whipples, and if they started at nine in the morning they
would be done by lunch time.

"My dad is the most remarkable person I've ever met. Yet there's a part of him I don't quite understand. There were times when I was in need, and he wasn't there for me. I'd get mad at times and say, 'He has so much money, but he just sends me twenty-five dollars a week.' When I was in medical school, my roommate Elton and I lived in the 'hood in a ten-by-ten room. Elton slept on a box spring. I slept on the mattress. We felt like soldiers in boot camp.

"Over the years I discovered that my dad has his weaknesses and strengths. He rose so far in life from being a very, very poor child all the way up to being a top-notch surgeon and a sports hero and a figure practically bigger than life. My view is that he wasn't able to fill in the gap of such a steep upward climb. Something was missing—not in his talent, not in his natural-born ability but in his interaction with the sick ways of the world.

"I've learned that anything you say can and will be used against you, no good deed goes unpunished, and, yes, nice guys do finish last. This is the opposite of what my dad thought. He believed that having an open and pure heart, going by your feelings, having an aggressive notion of winning, respecting and embracing God— that was all you needed. When my mom died, it broke his heart and nearly broke his spirit. I saw the impact it had on him."

With new insight Mo said, "Sweetie, I feel a real understanding of your dad and you. There's something very special about both of you. From this room and the photo of Olivia, I feel a strong connection to the past. Strangely, to me, Olivia seems to represent a journey not yet begun."

Outside the library the young couple heard, "OK, let's sing 'Happy Birthday.' Come on, everyone."

Hillary and Mo exited the library and went into the living room, which was filled with Hillary's father's friends. Maya was at the older man's side, and they sang "Happy Birthday," accompanied by the Cajun three-piece band.

Hillary saw Maya press a large gold coin into the old man's palm and close his fingers over it. As "Happy birthday, dear Hillary" rang out, Mo saw tears form in the man's eyes, and she saw him wink at his son, as if to say, "I'm very proud of you."

Everyone clapped. King Cake was served, and everyone got a piece of this traditional Cajun treat. When Hillary, Jr., took his first bite, he felt something hard. It was a little plastic baby that symbolized Jesus.

Maya saw this and said, "You are the lucky one. With this trinket comes various privileges and obligations."

Hillary said, "Thanks, Maya," but then thought he already had enough privileges and didn't really want any more obligations.

Mo and Hillary held hands and felt very close to each other. As the party started to wind down, they found Maya, the birthday boy, and Pascal in the foyer. They said their good-byes and walked out into the warm night air. Hillary put his arm around Mo while they waited for the valet to retrieve Mo's little Benz.

On the way back to Hillary's apartment, he said to her for the second time that night, "Sweetie, I love you."

Mo felt herself respond from her heart. "I love you too."

They made it back to the apartment; he exited the car and walked around to the driver's side. Mo got out, and the two hugged and kissed each other good night. Hillary watched as Mo drove away, and then he walked up the fifteen steps to his apartment. As he checked the time on his phone—10:05 p.m.—in came a text from Mo. "I love you soooooo much. xoxoxoxoxo."

Smiling, he texted back, "I think I found my soul mate."

Once inside, the tired doctor thought about the next day's events. In a little less than eight-and-a-half hours, he had an aneurysm to repair. Then—groan—he had a trauma quality-improvement meeting at noon (a meeting he hated going to but knew was necessary, given the way *certain people* were). Next up, bedtime checklist: clothes off, teeth brushed, under covers, eyes closed.

CHAPTER 6

ᏀᎳᎵᎧ

The day began as Hillary exited his car and walked quickly through the doctors' parking lot into the hospital. As he walked, he reviewed the day's events. In twenty minutes he was scheduled to start the repair of a large abdominal aortic aneurysm. This was an elective operation. An aneurysm is a weakness in the layered wall of an artery, and in this case the aortic aneurysm was just below the renal arteries, which were in the back compartment of the abdomen.

Having spoken to the patient's family, he described the aneurysm as a weakness or a ballooning, as sometimes seen on the tire of a car. Like a balloon, if inflated too much, it could pop. If a person's aneurysm ruptured, the chance of death would be 50 to 99 percent, while an unruptured aneurysm could be repaired with minimal risks. In the past these aneurysms were repaired through major surgery, but now they could be repaired via an endovascular approach—a team-approach procedure with the placement of a self-expanding bypass graft with a stent.

Hillary thought this would be the easy part of his day. The hard part would be the quality-improvement meeting at noon. This was a scheduled trauma QI meeting that took place every month.

In saner circles, the QI meeting was a learning experience where docs on the trauma service could reflect on mistakes made and learn how not to make them again. QI was supposed to be a tool, not a weapon. Poor leadership at the administrative level, however, had been the catalyst for the "weaponization" of this meeting,

We docs are our own worst enemy, Hillary thought grimly. In particular, there was one doctor, the so-called alpha-male trauma surgeon, a former military doctor, who had an enormous ego, a ballistic temper, and an often-uncontrollable rage. For some reason, however, he was quite cozy with the hospital administration, and the trauma committee, which was also known as a peer-review committee, was immune to fair play.

In California, over a ten-year stretch, there had been thirty-three lawsuits in which doctors claimed that the peer-review process had been unfair to them. In fact it was so unfair that the doctors on the peer-review committee essentially had crucified the other doctors by telling lies and ruining their careers. In these thirty-three lawsuits, the particular doctors trying to protect their reputations had won only three times. The dirty little secret of medicine was that the self-governance and peer-review process was corrupt.

Hillary changed into scrubs and met Janelle and Henry. All three scrubbed and began the procedure. Hillary showed them how to do the procedure, and things went smoothly. At the end they spoke to the family, and everyone appeared relieved that the aneurysm had been safely repaired.

After finishing up the paperwork, the trio walked outside the main hospital building and headed toward the peer-review conference room. It was a nice day. The sun was beating down warmly; there were clear skies and a slight breeze. The grounds of the hospital were well kept, and since they were in L.A., "all walks of life" were present.

A radio-type noise came from Henry's coat pocket, and Hillary asked, "Is that a police scanner?"

Henry, somewhat of a computer buff and a would-be geek, despite his physical presence and height, responded, "Yeah, Doc, this is cool. I have this new scanner that scans the EMS, police, and fire, along with nine-one-one."

Janelle asked, "What's the deal with this peer-review process?"

Hillary explained, "It's a process where each month we're supposed to, in an educational manner, review the trauma cases where there was a complication and also review the patients who did not make it and decide whether their deaths were preventable, not preventable, or potentially preventable. Unfortunately several people use this process as a weapon and not a tool."

The meeting was due to start in about ten minutes, and already Hillary felt his stomach churning. Fortunately he hadn't had any complications this month and no mortalities. He felt comfortable that there wouldn't be any issues for him, but still he felt anxious.

Henry's scanner went off, and it was a 911 call. "Guys, listen to this," he said.

There were two long sounds and a short sound followed by, "Hello, nine-one-one."

On the other end of the line was the voice of a small child. He sounded like he was five or six years old. The small voice said, "Somebody shot Grandma and my mommy."

The 911 operator asked, "Is the person still there?" and the youngster said, "It was Daddy. My daddy came in and shot Grandma in the head and shot Mommy in the chest. Grandma isn't moving, and Mommy is saying, 'Help me! Help me!' "

The 911 operator tried to regroup herself. Fortunately Los Angeles had enhanced 911, which meant the address of the caller came up automatically. She issued dispatch orders to LAPD, L.A. Fire, and the paramedics.

The 911 operator asked the little one, "What's your name?"

The boy said, "My name is Junior."

"Junior, I want you to stay here with me on the phone, OK? Help is on the way." About ninety seconds later, the 911 operator saw on her screen that the police department was 10-97 (radio code for "on scene"). This was followed by 10-55 (coroner needed), which meant there was a dead body. After confirming that the PD was on scene, the operator said, "Junior, the police officer is going to take care of you, and the paramedics will take care of your mommy."

Junior said, "Thank you, ma'am," and hung up.

Junior displayed wisdom beyond his years and was a very brave lad. The backdrop to exactly what had happened had started several hours earlier when Junior's mom and grandmother were at home, and Elfand, the father of Junior and the estranged husband of the mother, had threatened the three of them. Several minutes earlier the father had returned and burst into the house enraged, screaming multiple epithets. In a mindless act, he pulled out an AK-47 and shot the grandmother in the head and his wife in the chest.

Henry, Janelle, and Hillary were listening to the scanner, their ears essentially glued. Hillary's phone rang, and his pager went off at the same time. He looked at the pager and saw Mo's number. The phone rang again. "Hey, sweetie," he said. "What's up?"

"Hill, I'm at your dad's house," she said. "Maya called and said your dad was having trouble breathing. Overall he looks OK, but he's having some trouble with his ventilator, so I called nine-one-one. The paramedics and ambulance are coming to take him to the emergency room. He should be there in about fifteen minutes."

Hillary felt the pressure of his day increase by 100 percent. "OK, Mo," he said. "I'll meet you there."

He turned to Janelle and Henry, "Man, oh, man, you just can't tell what is going to happen in a day. My dad is having some trouble with his vent, and he's coming to the emergency room. He should be here in about fifteen or twenty minutes, so let's catch a little bit of the meeting, and then we'll have a good reason to leave."

The meeting started at noon sharp. The time was 12:05, and already the alpha-male, dirtball trauma surgeon was in high gear. His object of torture today was a neurosurgeon, Dr. Guroz, age sixty-six, gray-haired, almost bald, and near the end of his career; Dr. Guroz was a gentleman through and through.

Dr. Puler tore into the man. "Look, you made a mistake. You killed this patient. It's well and true—just goddamn admit it."

He continued his brutalized personal attack. Dr. Guroz was just like a boxer who had gone beyond his ability to defend himself, but tried to anyway. This QI meeting quickly turned out to be one of the worst examples of how doctors got along with one another. Fortunately the meeting was interrupted by Dr. Puler's beeper going off, followed by the trauma phone ringing.

Dr. Puler announced, "Look, I can't stay here anymore. I'm on trauma call, and I have a trauma coming in right now, so it's fortunate for you that I have to leave, but make no mistake, we'll pick this up at our next meeting."

Janelle was particularly affected by Dr. Puler's behavior. It reminded her of how her father used to scream at her, her twin brother, and her mom. She could still hear her mom's voice as she cried out, "They're only kids," and pled for mercy.

Henry, Hillary, and Janelle exited on the heels of Dr. Puler. Hillary asked Dr. Puler, "Hey, Doc, what's coming in?"

Sarcastically Dr. Puler replied, "Why do you care? You're not on trauma call. It's probably something you couldn't handle, since you're not a critical care surgeon like me. If you must know, it's some lady who was shot in the chest and is coming in with barely any vital signs. She should be here in about ten minutes. I'm going to the cafeteria to get me some lunch before this all starts."

Henry, Hillary, and Janelle all looked at one another at the same time. They put two and two together, and Hillary exclaimed, "Holy smoke." This must have been the 911 call they had heard on Henry's scanner. Junior's little voice and the innocent words "Thank you, ma'am" had nearly brought tears to their eyes. The little kid's touching words, compared to Dr. Puler's cruel, sarcastic rant, made Hillary, Henry, and Janelle think Dr. Puler was a selfish, narcissistic individual.

Janelle couldn't contain herself. Being the closest of the docs to her psych rotation, she retorted, "I bet Dr. Puler carries the DSM-three-approved diagnosis 'malignant narcissist.' " All agreed as they quickly walked to the emergency room.

Mo called one last time. "Hillary," she said, "We're in the emergency room. It's completely full. We'll be in the trauma room."

Hillary picked up the pace, took a deep breath, and told Mo, "We'll be there in ninety seconds."

Hillary, Henry, and Janelle entered the trauma room through its internal entrance. The room was able to accommodate two patients at the same time, although it was usually a tight squeeze. As Mo, Hillary Sr., and the paramedics entered, all eyes fell on the wide-eyed, anxious patient with ALS.

Two paramedics from Engine Company 97 were watching over the good doctor. There was no sign of the patient's home vent; he was hooked up to an Ambu bag that was attached to the tube coming out of his throat. The life-supporting trach tube appeared to be open, and the patient seemed to be getting enough air and oxygen.

Somehow Engine 97 had been able to load Hillary, Sr., and his wheelchair with all its bells and whistles into the ambulance.

The medic gave a report to Hillary. He said he thought the problem had been with the patient's battery and A/C connection. Hillary quickly listened first to his dad's lungs, then to his heart tones. "Ah, yes. S-one, S-two, no S-three, and no S-four—no muffled heart tones, no sign of fluid around the heart. Great, Dad."

After his quick exam, Hillary felt comfortable that airway, breathing, and circulation were all intact. The respiratory therapist brought in a vent, and Hillary, Jr., shook his head and thought what a shame it was to be stricken with this paralyzing, god-awful disease. Recalling the home vent settings, he said, "Hook him up to the vent, tidal volume six hundred, assist-control of twelve, fraction of inspired oxygen forty percent."

Once it appeared that his father was stable, Hillary attached the plug from the home retinal scanner to the back of one of the hospital computers that was connected to a large monitor on the wall. The monitor was as large as a big-screen TV. The retinal scanner was working, so even though the older doc had yet to embrace the technology, Hillary told his dad, "In case you want to, you're hooked up. See, I can even type you a message… 'I love you.'"

Henry, Janelle, and Mo could all see that Hillary, Sr., was scared. The stricken doc silently wondered, *Is this my last hurrah?*

Molly, one of the ER nurses, came in and saw that Dr. Chollet had hooked his dad up to the vent. She said, "Hey, you guys did everything already. In a few minutes, we have a bad trauma coming in, so you'll all have to sit tight." Molly looked at the three docs, Mo, and the still semi-panicked patient. Satisfied, she said to Hillary, Sr., "I can see you're in good hands." She checked out Mo from top to bottom and wondered whether she was the one who would capture Hillary's heart.

Janelle held the stricken doctor's left hand while Mo held the right one.

A minute later the page operator announced, "707 in two minutes."

Third-year resident Henry, still on the vascular service with Hillary, was so excited he could hardly stand it. He knew Dr. Puler was on call, however, and that there was little to no chance that he would be able to help. Dr. Puler always did everything himself.

The ER ambulance entrance was nearby, so everyone in the trauma room heard the siren of the incoming unit. A final sign, heard as the ambulance hit the emergency room ambulance bay, was the backup sound, *Beep, beep, beep, beep.*

Next was the sound of the gurney's wheels as they skated down the hallway and into the trauma room. On arrival was a near-dead black woman, who in fact was the mother of the child who had made the 911 call. "Crashing" before everyone's eyes, she was essentially dead, having lost her blood pressure and all her vital signs. Hillary looked around but saw no sign of Dr. Puler. Henry looked at Hillary; Hillary looked at Janelle, who then looked at Mo. Mo looked at Hillary, Sr., whose eyes had grown wide. Now stable, he was the observer, not the observed.

The nervous ER nurse paged Dr. Puler. "Dr. Puler to the emergency room STAT." The ambulance stretcher rolled up next to the ER stretcher.

Finally, Dr. Puler showed up and told everyone, "OK, I'm in charge here. What do we have?"

The senior paramedic rolled his eyes, and rightly so, as the medics were the ones who created order from disorder and made just 7 percent of the preventable mistakes in trauma. This particular medic had twenty years more experience than Dr. Puler.

Quickly the junior paramedic said, "We have a twenty-nine-year-old woman who was at home. An intruder came in and shot her in the chest with an AK-forty-seven. Just as we were unloading her, she lost all her vital signs and essentially has no blood pressure."

This was a high-visibility case already, and outside the hospital, network TV trucks were arriving. They probably had found out what had happened the same way Henry, Janelle, and Hillary had, with "not-supposed-to-have" police scanners. It was even possible ambulance chasers were on the way too. Molly hooked the patient up to the monitor and confirmed that she had no vital signs. CPR was started on the woman.

Dr. Puler said, "I think I feel a pulse. Let's give her some blood."

Also part of the trauma team was the ER doctor, who confirmed that the breathing tube was in place. He did a FAST exam (focused ultrasound assessment) and said, "Doc, she's got blood around her heart, and I see minimal to no activity."

Like a hive brimming with bees, the trauma room filled with both helpers and gawkers. Even the chief of surgery came into the room. He was a world-famous vascular surgeon, who, over the years, had worked with the senior Hillary and had taken the younger Hillary under his wing after his Vascular Surgery fellowship in Philadelphia.

Dr. Puler looked at the patient, then at the ER doctor, and said, "I have to crack this lady's chest."

He retrieved a scalpel as the nurse squirted Betadine on to the woman's chest. He lifted her left breast, made a slash incision in the crease over the fifth rib, and cut through the muscles between the ribs. Next he put a retractor in place and cranked open the chest, found her heart had stopped, and started to massage the empty non-beating heart. He said, "This is really bad. I don't know if there's any hope."

The chief of surgery, himself a vascular surgeon, said, "Open up the pericardium, Dr. Puler."

"OK."

Dr. Puler took a pair of Metzenbaum scissors, and with hands trembling, he opened up the pericardium and noted there was blood inside, which signified a gunshot to the heart. He squeezed the heart, sort of fumbling as he did, but couldn't find the hole in the heart.

"I can't see anything. There's so much blood. There's no hope here. I think we should call it."

The chief of surgery knew what each surgeon was capable of. He also happened to know Dr. Puler's strengths and weaknesses and decided to make a change. Looking straight at the younger Hillary, the chief said, "Chollet, you take over."

Like an understudy in the theater, the replacement trauma surgeon had been called in, and without reservation Hillary realized it was up to him. Henry nearly jumped out of his skin over the prospect of trying to save this young lady. Janelle had seen so much over the past few weeks that she was just holding on tight on this roller coaster of emotion, drama, and learning.

Hillary looked at Henry and Janelle and said, "OK, guys, we're up."

Dr. Puler stepped aside as Hillary, Henry, and Janelle assumed their positions.

Donning size seven-and-a-half gloves, Hillary reached into the left chest through the thoracotomy incision. Then he cranked the retractor open a few extra turns to allow for better exposure. "Let's see what we have here," he said.

The mood of the entire room changed. A head surgeon is like an orchestra leader—or a composer—someone who sets the tempo and is able to make people work with encouragement and praise rather than ridicule and harsh words. Every once in a while, the composer must tap his stick to make the musicians pay attention, but in general it's a cohesive, coordinated effort.

As Hillary slipped his hand into the chest, he saw several of the OR nurses, including his buddy Virgil, arrive, so he invited them onto the field. They instinctively added additional drapes to prevent infection. Standing at the head of the patient, the anesthesia doctor now felt more comfortable.

Even though this young lady had no vital signs, hope was still present. Hillary fully delivered the heart outside of the pericardium (the sac around the heart) and felt two holes in the left ventricle through and through. He supported the heart with his right hand and, by gentle feel with his right index finger, found and plugged the hole at the back of the heart. He placed the index finger of his left hand inside the hole in the front part of the heart and gently massaged the heart. This gave him a little time—about twenty seconds—to assess the situation and also allowed some time for the massive transfusion protocol and the infusion of fluids and uncross-matched blood. With a plan in place, he was ready.

A testing of blood from an artery—ABG—came back and showed a pretty severe acid buildup, but it also showed that the patient had good oxygenation. Her hemoglobin came back at 4 g, normal being 12 to 14 g. Uncross-matched blood and fresh frozen plasma were given, and Hillary felt the heart start to fill.

He said to his third-year resident, "Henry, we don't have much time." Like an expert chess player, he was thinking a couple of moves ahead. "Her heart is going to start in less than two minutes, and we have to get these holes closed. Henry, put your finger in this hole on the front part of the heart. We're going to lift the heart up, and I'm going to whip in some stitches."

Henry followed the order, and the trauma vascular surgeon, now with "quiet eyes," said, "Give me a three-oh Prolene suture, and make it a pledgeted suture." A pledget is a small piece of Teflon. The size of two peas placed side by side completely flat, it's used as a belt or bolstering of the stitch so that it doesn't tear through when tied down.

The nurse said, "Doctor, we don't have any pledgets."

Hillary told Janelle, "While I'm getting ready, I want you to make me some pledgets from the pericardium."

The chief of surgery felt a bit nostalgic because that was a trick he had taught Hillary when he was an intern some eight years ago.

The pledgets were ready, and the heart was lifted out of the chest. With a finger in the front hole, two figure-eight pledgeted sutures were placed, and the hole was closed. Gently the heart was returned into the chest. Hillary removed Henry's finger and replaced it with his own finger. Additional volume was given, and the heart started to fill quickly. Hillary made sure there was no air in the heart; if there were, an embolus could occur and cause a stroke. He placed two more pledgeted sutures, making sure the coronary artery wasn't snagged by a stitch. The last stitches were readied for tie-down, and all air, blood, and debris was allowed to exit. Then he tied down the stitch and felt a single beat of the heart. Everyone in the room was ecstatic, except for Dr. Puler, who secretly hoped the patient wouldn't make it.

Hillary asked the anesthesia doctor, "What's her temp?" and an esophageal recording revealed that the temperature was eighty-eight degrees Fahrenheit—well below the actual normal temperature of 98.6. He knew that as a person cooled off, there was an increased risk of irritability on the heart, and at eighty-seven to eighty-eight degrees Fahrenheit, the heart actually could stop. Supporting this patient's heart by compressions, Hillary gently pressed it enough to give a blood pressure of around sixty systolic.

"Give me some warm saline," he said. "I need two liters of warm saline."

Several liters of toasty warm saline were delivered, and Hillary said, "Pour it into the chest. Pour it over the heart. We have to warm this lady up."

After the first liter, another spontaneous heartbeat took place. After the second liter, there seemed to be a little more activity, with about four beats per minute. Having been in this situation before, the anesthesia doctor said, "I'm giving calcium and magnesium."

Hillary quickly nodded in agreement. The whole room grew silent. There was now a completely cohesive arrangement with at least twenty people working, and even Dr. Puler was peeking onto the operative field. Hillary called for an additional liter of warm saline. It filled up the left chest, and the saline started to bubble over and went onto the floor. The patient's heart rate increased, and not unexpectedly so, she started to fibrillate. Fibrillation (ventricular variety) is a severe arrhythmia that doesn't allow the heart to send oxygenated blood to itself or to the brain. Treatment is delivered through paddles and defibrillation.

In this case, since the heart was exposed, Hillary said, "Give me the internal paddles. Thirty joules, please." Holding the paddles with insulated handles, he shocked the patient once, but she was still fibrillating. Calm and in the moment, the doc inspected the cardiac repair.

"Sweet," Henry said.

Hillary said, "Forty joules, and if her heart starts, then seventy-five milligrams of lido." He placed the paddle in his left hand on the front of the heart and the right-hand paddle behind the heart. The fibrillating heart, squirming like a thousand worms all at once, needed to be shocked into submission. The shock would temporarily overwhelm the heart and stop all electrical heart activity, allowing the heart to reboot.

Hillary instructed everyone to "clear." Once he was sure no one was touching the patient, he pressed the buttons on each handle and delivered the shock. The patient and heart jumped a little as the shock was delivered—Vfib (shock); then flat line for one second; then *beep, beep*...then her heart started.

Everyone cheered.

Just as her heart started, however, Hillary, who was holding the paddles, happened to be standing in a quarter-inch of water and blood. He got electrocuted from a short in the paddle in his right hand. He received forty joules, but his standing in water and blood magnified the conduction. He was so electrified that as the young woman's heart started, his heart stopped.

He let go of the paddles as the explosion of electricity entered his right palm and surged throughout him. It went up his arm, through his chest and heart, down his left leg, and then exited through the sole of his foot. With his heart stopped, he started to fall backward.

CHAPTER 7

⟨≈≈≈⟩

Hillary had been caught by surprise. The situation quickly worsened, as all the oxygenated blood that was supposed to go to his brain stopped flowing. The doctor's right hand was still smoking from the defib burn, and a quarter-sized black spot started to appear on the palm of his right hand and the sole of his left foot. This signified the course that the electric current had taken. Both his hand and foot and everything in between burned like fire. It all had happened so fast—heart stopped no oxygen, and no control of circumstance. He fell backward; just past the forty-five degree angle, he blacked out.

After he was out for perhaps a few seconds, his eyes opened, and he found himself floating above his body. A surreal feeling took hold as this new perspective provided a unique view of the trauma room. He was able to see everything and everyone, and for a moment, all action in the room stopped. Like in a cartoon, time screeched to a halt—but just for half a second, as everyone jumped back into action amid this incredulous circumstance.

The trauma room had sixteen-foot ceilings, and as Hillary floated out of his body near the ceiling, his eyes landed on the woman who had been shot in the heart. From above he peered into her chest and saw that her heart was beating nicely. Also visible were the sutures he and Henry had placed.

The heart monitor showed stable vital signs: blood pressure 118 over seventy, heart rate 110 with a normal-looking tracing of sinus rhythm. Visible on the floor were the fallen defibrillator paddles. Hillary thought, *It looks like she's going to make it.*

More and more people crammed into the trauma room after Hillary had passed out. The first to reach him was his friend, Dr. Bruce Cummings. An ER doctor for twenty-five years, he knew the routine and quickly inserted a breathing tube into his friend's throat. Once the tube was in, Dr. Cummings listened to each lung to confirm good breath sounds.

The respiratory therapist hooked Hillary up to 100 percent oxygen and an Ambu bag, and the still out-of-body Hillary thought he could help himself by taking a deep breath. Then he wondered, *How can an out-of-body deep breath possibly help me?*

A new reality played out as his "taking a breath" made him feel no better or worse. Multiple people, in a very rough way, grabbed his limp body and dragged it onto a gurney. Dr. Puler saw his opportunity and tried to retake charge of the woman who had been shot in the chest, but the chief of surgery thought otherwise and took over the case himself. He said, "Stand clear, Dr. Puler. I'm taking her to the OR to close up her chest."

Pain and agony enveloped Hillary as he looked at the faces of his dad, Henry, Janelle, and Mo. His physical pain started to become more bearable, but his mental distress escalated. He saw the terror on Mo's face and wished she would float up next to him so he could tell her how much he loved her. He was so frustrated; his lips mouthed the words, "I love you, Mo."

As Hillary looked down on his body, and as the doctors and nurses worked on him, he started to feel different; he began to lose interest in his physical form.

The young female patient was close to being wheeled to the operating room. Above her gurney, Hillary looked at the clock and noted the time—1:00 p.m.—and, as he did, a warmth from behind his neck caused him to turn. He saw two white lights that were very bright but didn't hurt his eyes. One of the white lights enveloped his out-of-body form.

As a trauma and vascular surgeon, Hillary had treated patients who'd had near-death experiences, but this was the first time he'd had such an experience on "the other side of life." Swept up, he thought back to when he was a little kid and first got on a roller coaster. Back then, just as the coaster started, his mind had told him, *This doesn't seem too scary.* A similar thought popped into his mind now as he started to become excited in a kidlike way. He said to himself, *Some people would die to have this experience.*

The white light completely enveloped him as the feelings of readiness and excitement built up. As he was full of white-light expectations, confusion also ensued. No music, no end to the white light, no sign of his mom, no beautiful gardens, no trumpets. What was the deal? Was this a typical white-light experience?

Slightly bewildered, he felt himself drawn up the white-light tube. It went through the ceiling and created an exit from the trauma room. Next to him was a second white-light tube that touched his. The thought occurred, *Maybe I'm in the wrong one. No, that's crazy.* After several seconds of ascension, into view came an object coming down the other lit tube. He said out loud, "She's a beautiful woman. Who is this woman? It's my patient!"

Only six feet away, smiling as she approached, her figure turned toward Hillary. Like two people passing on opposite escalators—one up, one down—their eyes met, and a tear rolled down her left cheek and stopped at her chin. She reached through her white light into Hillary's white light and touched his face. He was able to see but could not hear as she mouthed the words, "Thank you."

So many times in the doc's career, the words "Thank you" had been heaped upon him, and he felt there was no greater compliment than those two words of gratitude heard from survivors of trauma, accidents, limb-salvage operations, and cancer surgeries.

He remembered the time a man had lost his wife from a ruptured aortic aneurysm. After the news, the man had said he felt bad *for Hillary*. "Don't feel bad, Doc," he had said. "You tried your best. Thank you."

"Thank you" was an honor when spoken. The highest honor in medicine was the implied trust given, when a patient was too unstable to say "yes" or "no." The honor of this trust was the privilege of treating everyone the same—whether it was the bank president or the town drunk; this highest honor carried the obligation of being impartial and treating everyone the same.

Hillary savored the mouthed thank-you as this beautiful woman—his trauma patient—headed down the white light back to the OR and trauma room. *It looks like she's going to survive,* he thought. *Hooray!*

As he headed in the opposite direction, he wondered what fate held in store for him. His patient had vanished into the silhouette of her descending white light. The doctor ascended faster through his white light. At first he went straight, but then the lit tube took a turn. Was this a wormhole? Once again, no music. There were no kids playing, and he didn't see his mother. Was this a mistake? Hillary wasn't able to attach a definite amount of time to this transport, but after a while, his movement slowed down, and the white light started to dim. Then everything went dark.

CHAPTER 8

❦

As the light turned into darkness, quietness set in, and Hillary thought he could hear his own heartbeat.

Am I alive? he wondered.

After a minute or so of darkness, things lightened up, and he tried to regain his bearings. He could now see his outstretched hand; a quick exam revealed he was still standing in his scrubs, the same clothes he had worn in the trauma room—the same shoes and even the same blood-soaked surgical booties.

The surroundings were dark and dusky, as if it were after sunset. No sign of sun, moon, or stars. He saw people thirty to forty yards off to his right but couldn't see their faces. Rows and rows of stadium-type folding chairs, all empty, gave the perception that this was some sort of huge holding area. Off to the left was a wall, and from this shadowy, near-nighttime arena came a voice that said, "Stay in line. Stay in line. This way. This way. Stay in line. Stay in line."

Hillary gravitated toward the sound, and into view came a long line of people in single file. Trepidation and a slight fear took hold as he saw the line of people taper off into darkness. Not more than thirty feet behind the last person in line, an individual suddenly came from the left. He seemed to be one of the people in charge and said to Hillary, "Hold on a second. You don't belong here. You belong over there," and he pointed in the opposite direction.

Hillary turned and looked to where the man pointed. He saw an enormous white light. The stranger said, "Tell you what. Walk down about two hundred yards and take a left."

As Hillary listened, he noticed the stranger's friendly face and long white robe and eyes that seemed full of goodness. A thought popped into his mind as he thanked him. *Is this an angel?* If so, maybe a "God bless you" would have been smarter.

Still in the arena, Hillary walked toward the white light. After a few hundred yards, the long wall on his left ended, and he took a left-hand turn as directed. The landscape took on a noticeable change, and before him was a beautiful street illuminated by white light. He saw a cobblestone street with a Tuscan-village feel. The path before him was lined with structures that looked like storefronts. There were no people, no flowers, no typical signs of life or activity. *Am I imagining all this?* Hillary wondered.

Each store had a picture window with closed, decorative colored curtains and a door. The storefronts were connected to each other, and the street extended as far as the eye could see. Above each door was a little window smaller than the width of the door but only five or six inches high.

Hillary felt a cool breeze across his face and wondered whether he was indoors or outdoors. Still in his scrubs, he walked onto the cobblestone and felt the rounded stones under his feet. He looked at the storefronts, and as he turned and faced the first one on his right, the window above the door lit up. He looked across the street, then down the road for quite a ways but didn't see any other lit windows. Visible in big block letters were the words SAINT HILARY OF POITIERS.

He walked toward the door; it seemed natural to enter. Hillary tried to remember how to address a saint and also wondered whether he should knock. He played it safe by knocking twice and then twisting the doorknob. Once inside he found a small room, perhaps as small as a vestibule. Sitting down was a man of the church—a saint! He invited Hillary in and offered him a seat. The saint was dressed regally, even more so than the Pope on Christmas Day at the Vatican. He was wearing a red cape with gold trim, and a tall, white peaked cap. This saint had olive-colored skin, jet-black hair, and no facial hair or visible blemishes. His face was round in shape. The saint spoke in French, and despite Hillary not understanding French—except the little he had learned in junior high—somehow every one of the man's insightful, articulate words were familiar and easy to understand. He handed Hillary his calling card that read, "Saint Hilary of Poitiers, Doctor of the Church." He then began a conversation that would change Hillary's life—or whatever this little bit of existence represented.

The saint spoke with an air of omniscience as he laid down some historical groundwork.

He spoke eloquently, starting with Abraham, and then he switched from BC to AD, and with pride and love talked about Jesus, the Prince of Peace. Saint Hilary's discourse arrived at the twentieth century, at which point he moved his head sideways the same way the doctor did when he barely could believe something that was incredulous but true.

"Hillary, I'd better get to the point," the saint said. "We need you." Next he asked a question in the same way an employer would ask a prospective employee without having first read his résumé. "Is this your first time, Doctor? Oh, never mind. It doesn't matter."

Saint Hilary reviewed the nature of the duality of the universe and free choice, and confirmed the reality of both light and dark forces. Then he started to explain the mission. He seemed to unlock all the areas of Hillary's mind. Hillary wasn't afraid, but he was sad for his family and for Mo; his past existence started to seem far away. He felt as though he were able to reach into every part of his mind; suddenly into focus came the words "We need you." Hillary thought, *Who are "we"?*

The saint expressed his understanding of Hillary's pre-white-light experience. As if the two were both looking with the same eyes and listening with the same ears, a brief recap of the ER events replayed—this time without sound and with sympathetic, nonverbal expressions from the saint.

The saint's introspective responses transcended the traditional verbal explanation in first person, second person, or third person. Without words he sent thoughts, sounds, and feelings into Hillary's mind, which gave him new understanding.

CHAPTER 9

Hillary reviewed the typical stages of loss, including denial, anger, grief, and acceptance, and was semi-mystified by how he had gone from denial to acceptance so quickly.

As he looked at Saint Hilary, he remembered from college that this saint was born around 300 AD to pagans of distinction and later studied Christianity and was baptized. Augustine of Hippo had called him "the illustrious Doctor of the Churches."

How could someone so old look so good?

Saint Hilary asked the doctor to hold out his hands, palms up. With his right hand, he reached for Hillary's palm and with his thumb and forefinger together, he pulled out something that expanded into a one-foot-tall hologram. Then Saint Hilary said, "These are the Strings of Life."

The young doctor added, "That's the DNA helix."

The saint nodded. Then he revealed that the entire existence of humanity was encoded in this double-stringed double strand. Next the Doctor of the Churches touched Hillary's left palm, and he saw another one-foot-tall hologram—a crown of wiggling strings next to the DNA helix. The good saint said to Hillary, "I know you are a doctor and a scientist. Do you recognize this?"

Hillary, who had gone through four years of college, four years of medical school, and an additional seven years of training, never had seen anything like this. Vaguely he remembered seeing a diagram of these little strings in a science magazine and wondered if they were related to string theory and the theoretical notion that humans exist in eleven dimensions, not just three.

Saint Hilary read his mind and said, "Very good, Doctor. These are the Strings of Time." Feelings of wonderment, amazement, comfort, and awe swirled around and through Hillary. The saint said, "Look at these Strings of Life. The arrangement includes a coding of all of humanity from beginning to end. Let me give you an example." Another hologram appeared; it was a multidimensional movie of a swimming tadpole.

Hillary wondered, *Is this saint an angel? Is this saint…God? Or is he a representative of God?* He remembered the long street with multiple doors and an area above each door. Was there a different saint behind each door?

The swimming tadpole started to grow and turned into a tadpole with legs. Then it grew even bigger, and after four or five transformations, it turned into a frog. This image disappeared, and an image of a womb appeared. Hillary thought back to his earliest memory, when he was a baby. He remembered his mother and how she had felt when he took her lipstick and made beautiful art on the walls.

Inside this womb was a child nearly ready to come out. As a doctor, he knew the signs of a baby being ready for birth. A new holographic movie started. The development regressed, and the baby grew smaller and smaller and smaller. Still inside the womb, the baby shrank down to an embryo with a tadpole-type tail. That picture disappeared, and the saint said, "Doctor, I know you understand this, but it's important that I reinforce this notion. Ontogeny recapitulates phylogeny. You know what that means, Doctor. Don't you?"

Hillary said, "Yes, sir. Every species begins with an egg and proceeds. Growing to an embryo and then to viability, the human being seems to be a summation of all of the creatures that have been created as its development goes from an egg to a complex of cells to something with a tail and then to a human being."

Saint Hilary said, "That's correct. This brings us to the present. We need your help. Actually I'm a little embarrassed as a saint to say that we had to make this arrangement, as it may be seemingly harsh for you."

The doctor accepted his fate and asked, "How can I help you?"

"There are forces of good and evil, a duality in life and free will. There is a child you need to help. This child has a providence that is not known."

Hillary needed more information and asked, "OK, who is the child? What can I do?"

Saint Hilary of Poitiers confessed, "I really can't say much more. What I can say is that the tools on the side of Light are faith, hope, courage, and love."

These words hit Hillary in a very challenging way. He processed them, but they seemed counterintuitive to his old way of survival. The saint then reached toward the crown of strings. He chose one of them and pulled it like a little worm; he took the string and moved it toward the double-string DNA helix next to it. The String of Time touched the two Strings of Life, and they melded into a new complex, and with that the saint touched the complex. It shrank, and he returned it to Hillary's open left hand. He then said, "This is all you need."

Saint Hilary reached into his pocket, removed a small round box, and revealed its contents. Hillary saw a large coin, bigger than a silver dollar; it appeared to be made of gold and was the most beautiful coin he ever had seen. Saint Hilary handed him the coin, and he looked at it closely. One side of the coin displayed a picture of the cosmos; on the other side was an actual picture of God. In Hillary's eyes this God appeared to be Jesus, but then a feeling went through him that this picture of God might appear different to different people.

Saint Hilary then took the closed box and twisted the bottom one-half turn clockwise, then one turn counterclockwise. This caused a little hidden drawer to pop open. He then placed another of his cards inside the drawer and slid it shut, and with a heavenly smirk said, "You might need to contact me."

After he handed the coin and box to Hillary, he added, "You will be transported to a time and place that you do not know. Your mission involves helping this child. Beyond that I cannot say more except to tell you to use the tools of the Light side: faith, hope, courage, and love. When you are satisfied that you have found the correct person, give him or her this coin." Saint Hilary added some encouragement. "You will see me again, once this task has been completed. It may take some time. Do not lose hope, do not lose faith, be courageous, and appreciate that we love you."

At the opposite end of the vestibule, a new door appeared, and without hesitation the doctor stood up, thanked the good saint, shook his hand, and considered what awaited him.

The brave doctor stepped through the door and then fell into a slumber.

CHAPTER 10

◖✺◗

Hillary found himself in front of a door that appeared to be the side door of a church. Fully aware, he was holding a suitcase and dressed as a priest in a dark suit and a clerical collar. Within earshot were the sounds of children playing. He also heard the trumpet sound of jazz music, a song he vaguely remembered coming from the 1930s. On the doorstep was a newspaper, which he picked up and opened. He had trouble believing the headline—"Hitler Rallies His Forces." A glance at the upper-right-hand corner showed the date to be August 4, 1938. The newspaper was the *New Orleans Daily*. "Holy smoke!" he said, as he wondered, *What the heck is going on?*

Behind the door of the church rectory, he heard some rustling. There was laughter and giggling, and then the door opened. Before him stood a priest and behind him, peering over his shoulder, were three nuns, all dressed in habits.

The priest wore gold-rimmed spectacles. He seemed jovial, with animated arms, and appeared to be about sixty years old. He was balding on top and had white hair on the sides. He said, "You must be Father Andrew. Thank you for coming to help us. We never thought we would be able to find both a coach and a math teacher to replace Father Peter, who so suddenly passed away. My name is Father Solomon, and these are Sisters Mary, Madeline, and Margaret. We call them 'the three M sisters.' "

They all laughed, including Father Andrew. Hillary couldn't help feel a bit of their warmth immediately. Standing there, taking stock, he thought back to what had just happened to him earlier. Was it only several minutes ago? Or longer? He *had* been talking with Saint Hilary. Was that a dream? Which scenario was reality? Was this reality? Or was that reality?

Still lingering was a faint memory of what had happened before his meeting with the saint, but for some reason this memory now resided in the deepest part of his being. Maybe it was for the best—a safety valve of sorts, perhaps. He felt sure he could access those and other memories if necessary. What had emerged were a new purpose and willingness to explore the moment at hand. He was now Father Andrew...

Father Andrew looked at his shoes, which he was pleased to note were nicely polished. He felt the soft fabric of his dark suit then reached up to his neck to the stiff clerical collar. The newly arrived priest looked at Father Solomon, and as if he were looking in a mirror, he saw his own priestly reflection.

Father Solomon and the three sisters welcomed him again and invited him in. He carried his suitcase in his right hand and the newspaper under his left arm. Sister Madeline walked up to Father Andrew, looked him in the eyes, bowed her head as if she were being obedient, and asked to carry his suitcase. As though invoking mores from a future time, Father Andrew felt Sister Madeline was his equal and said, "No, thanks, Sister. I'll carry my suitcase. It's a little heavy."

Father Solomon invited him into the rectory. He was clearly excited. "Father Andrew," he said, "put your suitcase down, and let me show you our church." He led the sisters and Father Andrew into the church through the front entrance, saying, "Let me give you the two-bit tour." He then decided to test his new math teacher. "Andrew, how much is 'a bit'?"

Two answers popped into his mind. First, two bits equal one byte. Second, one bit equals twelve-and-a-half cents. "Two bits equal twenty-five cents, Father."

Father Solomon smiled and continued his little tour of the church. Several minutes later they reached the altar, and all five dropped to their knees. Father Andrew overheard Father Solomon whisper, "Thank you, Lord, for bringing us Father Andrew."

All five stood and made the sign of the cross. Father Andrew took in a deep breath and tried to calm his nerves. They exited the church, and Sister Mary guided Father Andrew and his new friends down a long corridor lit by burning candles mounted on wall sconces until they returned to the rectory. Father Solomon invited Father Andrew to sit down as the three sisters headed into the kitchen and began to work on dinner. The elder priest asked him if would like something to drink.

Father Andrew answered, "Thank you. Water will be fine," but Father Solomon said, "Son, a moment like this deserves special attention, and for this I have a very special bottle of wine. It comes from Italy. It was bottled in eighteen seventy-five and was passed down to me from my mentor, Father Xavier. Since our parish, church, and school are in crisis, and now that the answer has arrived, it's time to celebrate."

Corkscrew in hand, Father Solomon popped the cork and filled two glasses halfway. He offered a toast. "To: our Father who art in heaven. Hallowed be thy name. And thank you for bringing Father Andrew to us."

Glasses touched, and then, as if he carried the weight of the world on his shoulders, Father Solomon told Father Andrew what his charge would be.

"Our church and high school are named Holy Cross, and we're in the Ninth Ward of New Orleans. Nineteen thirty-eight has been a tumultuous year. Many of the men have no work and hold a lot of fear over the fact that Germany is about to start a world war. This church in the Ninth Ward is the center point of relief for solving problems. We serve all ages and all walks of life. I'm so happy you're here, Father Andrew. As you know, you'll be the high school football and basketball coach and also our freshman and junior mathematics teacher. In addition you'll mentor boys in the seventh and eighth grade."

Father Solomon further explained that there seemed to be a multigenerational pattern in this part of New Orleans. This was true in the Ninth Ward particularly, where men married women and had children; when the men couldn't find jobs, they left. As part of the Depression generation, some of the young people became hoodlums.

Father Andrew began to understand the magnitude of his charge, and although he couldn't exactly remember his own childhood, he felt comfortable that he knew the ins and outs of football, basketball, and high school mathematics.

His mind started to wander into an exhilarated maze of thought and all that had happened, so he looked down to quiet his eyes and took a sip of wine to try to create a disconnect.

Sister Mary announced, "Dinner is served."

The sisters brought in a feast of crawfish and very spicy rice with mussels, clams, and blackened Cajun sausages. Father Solomon and Father Andrew and the three sisters had a nice time laughing and joking. By the end of dinner, Father Andrew could see that Father Solomon and the sisters had a single purpose, which was to hold this community together and to help intergenerational families exist and thrive.

Although somewhat of a card in his demeanor, Father Solomon turned serious. He told Father Andrew, "These young people need you. As their football and basketball coach and teacher of mathematics, you will have an opportunity to help mold their futures."

After a wonderful conversation and several glasses of wine, Father Solomon said, "You must be very tired after your journey. Let me show you your room. Since it's August, we're on summer break, but the day after tomorrow, summer training starts for football."

Father Solomon showed the worn-out young priest to his room and said, "We have a tradition here at Holy Cross. Each night the sisters and the priests put their shoes in front of the door of their room for polishing."

Father Andrew, suitcase in hand, thanked Father Solomon and bade him good night. The tired and slightly tipsy new priest entered his room, and with the help of the bright-yellow flame of an oil lamp, saw his desk, chair, and bed. Tired beyond his ability to even imagine what had happened this day, he said his prayers, unlaced and removed his shoes, put them outside the door, turned off the lamp, lay down on his new bed, and fell deeply asleep.

CHAPTER 11

❧

Father Andrew woke up at 6:00 a.m., and before his eyes opened, he wondered what kind of dream he'd had. Eyes open, he realized this was not exactly a dream.

Outside his window, birds were chirping, and he felt a slight breeze from the nearby ocean through the open window. Refreshed after a good night's sleep, Father Andrew surveyed the room: bed, desk, chair, mirror, and a basin with a pitcher of fresh water, along with several clean towels. Next to his bed was his suitcase. He looked in the mirror and into his own eyes.

"Gray hair at thirty-two. Already? Great."

Besides his age, the new priest remembered talking to Saint Hilary of Poitiers but didn't exactly remember *where* he had spoken to this high member of the church. Father Andrew's past seemed far away. The mission and reality of his exact situation were foremost on his mind.

He turned back to his suitcase and opened the container that held all of his worldly possessions. Not a large suitcase—two feet long, eighteen inches high, and eight inches deep—it was held closed by straps on either side of the handle. It was very old, which was evident from the numerous scratches in the leather, along with the dark stains that marred the original light-brown color. Andrew wished the old leather box could talk. He undid the straps, and inside he found a Bible, along with a journal and several articles of clothing. At the bottom sat a little round box. No bigger than four inches across, it almost looked like a tiny hatbox. Father Andrew removed the top of the box and found a gold coin inside.

He turned the box upside down and let the coin fall into his hand. A heavy gold coin, it was about three inches in diameter, and on one side it had a picture of what appeared to be the universe or cosmos. On the other side, there was a beautiful picture of Jesus. There was no date on the coin and no evidence from where it had come. He gave it a final look and feel, and then returned it to its box. As he did he remembered his charge from Saint Hilary. *A child has been born, but his faith and destiny have not yet been determined. When you are satisfied you have met the right individual, you are to give this coin to that person.*

Father Andrew washed his face and brushed his teeth with baking soda and water. A quick splash of water on his face, and he was ready for his day. In his suitcase he found a fresh T-shirt and underwear. He wore the same suit and clerical collar he had on yesterday; in his coat pocket was yesterday's newspaper. Andrew looked at the headline and date once again and could hardly believe his new situation. He remembered that Father Solomon had told him he would be the high school football and basketball coach and that he would teach mathematics to freshmen and juniors. He found his polished shoes, and once ready, headed down the hallway. He heard some rustling in the kitchen and found Sister Madeline humming away as she prepared breakfast.

Sister Madeline was thirty years old and had been a nun for about ten years. Born to missionary parents, she grew up in India where she had been educated. She was slim and had an angelic face and blonde tendrils that peeked out from beneath her headscarf. Along with the two other sisters and Father Solomon, she had been very worried about the future of Holy Cross Church and High School. Now that Father Andrew had arrived, they all felt much better.

"Good morning, Sister Madeline," the new father said.

Sister Madeline bowed her head. "Good morning, Father. Would you like some juice, a muffin, and fruit?"

The young priest thanked her, and they both sat down to enjoy breakfast. Father Solomon and the two other sisters arrived, and the senior priest again expressed his gratitude. "Andrew," he said, "we're so glad you're here. This is going to be a busy day, so we'll need a good breakfast."

After breakfast the sisters returned to their devotional area and began their prayers. Father Solomon headed to the front door of the rectory, grabbed his hat and a leather satchel, and told Andrew, "Here's a hat for you. This sun is very hot. It's the middle of summer, and you don't want to burn. I'm going to give you a tour of the city."

Once outside, Solomon asked with whimsy, "Do you want the red one or blue one?" Seeing Andrew's perplexed expression, the jokester priest pointed to two bicycles across the yard. Barely able to conceal his laugh, Andrew chose the red one, and they were off.

They exited the church onto Canal Street in the Ninth Ward of New Orleans and traveled down the road. The early-morning hustle and bustle of the city was underway. Everyone around the church waved to Father Solomon. First they went down by the docks, where longshoremen were processing their early-morning catch. Andrew noticed that Father Solomon seemed to know everyone. One of the fishermen came up to Father Solomon and handed him a package. Solomon reached for his wallet, but the fisherman refused to take his money. Inside the package was a nice selection of crawfish, shrimp, and mussels. Father Solomon gave his thanks, blessed the young fisherman, and put the gift inside his satchel. Then the two priests continued their bicycle tour of the city. Solomon once again thanked Andrew for coming. He added, "Tomorrow is Saturday, August sixth. It's the beginning of football season. The football program has been very important to Holy Cross High School."

Andrew knew the football season went from August all the way until November and that basketball season followed.

The two wound their way back toward the church, and as the sun struck high noon, they stopped at a corner in the French Quarter where an old woman was selling fruit. Solomon bought some bananas and oranges and blessed the old woman. As he paid her, Andrew could tell she was blind by the way she trustingly held out her hand and didn't bother to count the change. It was obvious Solomon had a legion of followers and friends and was an integral part of this community.

Back at the church, Solomon showed Andrew the high school and his classroom and took him to the athletic department and the football field. On the field by the clubhouse, Solomon spotted Nate, the assistant coach and trainer.

"Nate, I'd like to introduce you to Father Andrew, our new coach."

Nate was a Cajun-looking man, part white, part black, and part who-knew-what-else. As Nate reached out to shake hands, Father Andrew saw that he was missing his last two fingers. His skin was cracked, and he had many calluses; he clearly was a man who labored. Nate grabbed Andrew's hand and shook it with strength. In a deep-toned voice with a Cajun accent, he said, "Welcome, Father. I look forward to working with you."

Andrew felt an immediate connection with Nate and knew they would be fast friends for quite a long time. Father Solomon took Andrew back to the church. For the next few hours, they said their devotional prayers. "Every other Sunday," Solomon instructed, "you'll be reading the Bible passage and giving the homily for Sunday mass." It would be Andrew's turn to speak before the congregation in two weeks.

He reminded Andrew, "Tomorrow morning is the first day of football practice. It starts at eight sharp down on the field. There will be returning upperclassmen and incoming freshman, all of whom will be trying out. Players have to earn a position—no resting on past laurels. Our varsity football team will be limited to thirty-two players. Most of the other schools have forty-two, but we can only afford uniforms for thirty-two."

Andrew thanked Solomon. He had a new admiration for the older priest, who seemed to be loved by all. Solomon obviously had won the hearts of people far and wide through humor and what he previously had described as a learning style based on that of Jesus and Socrates.

Andrew realized that this man, Solomon, was quite a person. He returned to his room, opened his suitcase, and took out his journal. He wrote "August 5, 1938" and made note of the day's events. He decided this would help him develop a thought process for what would be a daunting task. As he finished his first journal entry, he heard a commotion inside the church.

The church was just a thirty-second walk from his room. Andrew used the altar as his vantage point. Halfway up the row of pews, he saw a screaming woman pinching a young boy's ear. Father Andrew quickly walked over to them and asked, "What do we have here?"

"Father, my name is Olga Chollet," the woman said, "and this is my youngest son, Hillary. He has two older brothers. Last year their father left. I don't know what to do with him. He won't listen to me."

Father Andrew surveyed the two and then asked the boy, "Son, how old are you?"

The kid said, "I just turned twelve, sir. My birthday is July twenty-fifth. I was born in nineteen twenty-six."

Father Andrew could tell they were poor. The woman was dressed in old clothes and already had gray hair. The skinny boy appeared to weigh about eighty-five pounds and had a Creole complexion. He had big ears and curly black hair and also wore tattered clothes: a shirt with missing buttons, pants with a belt that was a piece of rope, and no shoes.

The woman said, "I can't control this boy. Father, please help me."

Father Andrew sympathized with the woman and could tell she was at her wit's end. Straightaway he said, "Son, what's your full name?"

"Hillary Anthony Paul Chollet."

"Well, Hillary, I have an idea. Do you like football?"

This was essentially a rhetorical question because every young man, young boy, old man, and grown man—or for that matter, every woman, child, priest, and nun—in New Orleans loved football.

Hillary nodded, and Andrew continued, "Son, I want you to meet me on the football field tomorrow morning at eight. I want you to help me."

"I'm only going into the seventh grade," the boy said. "I'm not old enough to play high school football."

Father Andrew said, "We'll see about that."

This got Hillary's attention, and a smile came over his mother's face. Father Andrew added, "Son, get yourself some sneakers for tomorrow because there's going to be a lot of running."

Hillary said, "Yes, sir. I'll be there."

Olga thanked the priest, who in turn blessed them both. They turned around and walked toward the front of the church. Andrew took one last look at Hillary, who was already about four inches taller than his mother. It looked like he was going to be tall.

Father Andrew turned around and headed toward the altar. He stopped at the first pew and took in the beauty of this church; he gazed in awe at a fresco of *The Last Supper* and at another fresco of angels and saints.

Andrew was starting to feel the challenge before him. Turning back toward the many rows of pews, he became mesmerized by the fourteen Stations of the Cross along the walls. He looked at each one and felt their meaning. Eventually he turned back toward the large cross over the altar with Jesus on it, and the realization of what he had been called upon to do struck him to the core.

Father Andrew whispered to himself, "They need my help," and a heightened resolve took hold of him as he made the sign of the cross and then went down on both knees and thanked God for having trust in him.

Rising to his feet, Andrew decided to take a stroll through the rose garden. He began to process his day's experience; despite feeling the good Lord's trust, he questioned whether he was up to the task. A trickle of fear and nervous tension flowed into the conscious area of his brain and raised the thought, *What the heck am I doing here?*

Andrew tried to relax himself by pressing the webbed space between his thumb and index finger. Not sure how he knew this technique, he squeezed both hands—right then left—for five seconds each, to the point of a little pain. Then he let loose and felt his whole body relax. Once he felt calm, his mind refocused, and he understood why he was a bit scared. Something inside told him that besides Andrew's memory, there was a subconscious from another time inside him. From that sub-world came a haunted cry, "Help me."

Andrew tried to quantify this situation. "Now let's see," he mumbled to himself. "The body reacts the same way whether you're afraid, mad, in love, or watching a scary movie. The physiologic response is sweaty palms, dry mouth, and fast breathing along with an accelerated heartbeat. Physiologic arousal plus cognitive input equals emotion or feeling. If an emotion comes trickling from the subconscious of nineteen thirty-eight or whenever, if one subtracts the physiologic arousal, then we're left with the cognitive input that can be transferred to the conscious area and dealt with. $P + C = E$. $C = E - P$."

Andrew breathed a relaxed sigh and embraced his new meditative process and welcomed all incoming emotions. He decided that if the good Lord was backing him, he must be good enough. He meditated for an additional hour and then headed in for an early dinner, excited that tomorrow would be the first day of football season at Holy Cross High School.

CHAPTER 12

༄༺༒༻༄

Father Andrew woke at seven the next morning, and as he lay in bed, his eyes barely opened. Still very tired despite having had a good eight hours of sleep, he mused about his tiredness and thought perhaps it was the time change, but what time zone was heaven in—or wherever he had been two days ago?

Now mostly awake, he reviewed yesterday's events. He looked forward to today, since it was the first day of football season. The plan was to meet at the field at eight for football practice. Muscles still tight from yesterday's bike tour of the city, Andrew flopped out of bed and stretched his toned six-foot frame.

Rummaging through his suitcase, thinking it was time to un-pack, he said, "I'm staying" and slid into a pair of athletic shorts and a pair of white socks. Inside the closet he found a pair of football cleats that happened to be his exact size.

Andrew felt a two-day beard as he washed his face. He found a straight razor, something he had never used before. On the table next to his washbasin and mirror was a shaving brush and cream. Yesterday, when he had returned to his room, he noticed that his bed had been remade, and his dirty clothes had been washed and folded. He felt humbled by the kindness being extended his way.

Andrew lathered up and fortunately didn't cut himself with the straight razor. Face washed, teeth brushed, he was ready for the day.

He swung through the kitchen and took an apple and orange. It was early enough in the morning that Father Solomon wasn't up yet. The three sisters, however, had been up for several hours doing their meditative prayers. After Father Andrew exited the church, he sat on the top step of the walkway, pulled on his cleats, and double-tied his shoelaces. Standing up, he realized he was now Coach Andrew. Inside his pants pocket he found his whistle. A soft blow of the whistle signified the start of his coaching career.

Andrew headed to the football field, the hot sun already beating down. Despite a very slight cool breeze from the ocean, he felt the first few beads of sweat on his forehead. He walked past Canal Street and saw a black horse and buggy pass. Noisily offered was the *clip-clop, clip-clop, clip-clop* of the horse, its nostrils flared; it occasionally snorted as if it had been a long journey for both horse and driver. Andrew speculated how long his own journey would be.

As he neared the field, into memory came the church scene yesterday with the young boy and his mother. *Will he show up?* he wondered. Andrew arrived at the field by seven twenty, and already two people were there—Nate, his assistant coach, and the boy,

Hillary. Nate was arranging the equipment, and Hillary was gladly helping.

Andrew came up to the two and said, "Hi, guys. How's everything going?"

Nate replied, "It's going to be a great day, sir."

Hillary said, "Hello, Father. Thanks for asking me to help."

"You're welcome, son," Father Andrew said. "It's going to be hard work, but it'll be worth it."

Father Andrew and Nate looked at their new assistant—twelve years old with dark-brown eyes and skinny, muscular arms; they both saw a kid with spunk. Andrew felt humbled when he saw the shoes Hillary was wearing—sneakers at least two sizes too big with laces strapped around his skinny ankles; the shoes were torn, with loose pieces flopping in all directions. He thought, *They can't possibly even be hand-me-downs.* He didn't want to hurt the boy's feelings, but those shoes were so bad they looked like they had been picked from the trash.

"Hillary, you're twelve years old and starting the seventh grade. Ninth grade is when a boy is eligible to play football at Holy Cross, so for now you're going to be my assistant and Nate's assistant."

Nate chimed in, "Don't worry, sir. I'll take care of him."

Both Nate and Hillary had deep Cajun-colored skin. Side by side, Nate could have passed for Hillary's dad.

The young boy helped Nate unpack the football gear, and as eight o'clock arrived, thirty-five players showed up, their ages ranging from fourteen to seventeen. Football was extremely popular in New Orleans, and Holy Cross always put forth a good team.

Despite the school's location in a poor area of town, more often than not it was the talent and the desire that allowed Holy Cross to do well.

After all the boys arrived, Andrew said, "Boys, I'm your new coach, Father Andrew, and I look forward to working with you. I won't let you down, and I expect that you won't let the good Lord down and you won't let me down either." He half-jokingly added, "The good Lord loves football, and he loves seeing young men hard at work. OK, boys, enough small talk. Let's get to work." He blew his whistle. *Phweeeeeep!* "Give me ten one hundreds," he called out.

The boys let out groans because they all knew ten one hundreds meant running from goal to goal, which were a hundred yards apart, ten times. That meant one thousand yards or three thousand feet or two-thirds of a mile.

As they all walked to the goal line, Andrew said, "Hillary, I want you to run with the boys."

That's when some of the seniors decided they were going to pull a trick on the seventh grader.

Andrew said, "When I blow the whistle, you boys start."

A couple of the seniors came up to Hillary, and one of them said, "Boy, we're gonna give you a little bit of a head start, but if we catch you, we're going to pull your britches down!"

Hillary thought, *Holy smoke.* Although he had two older brothers, and from time to time felt tortured by them, he was truly scared.

The coach blew the whistle, and the boys started to run. Hillary blistered out ahead of every single one of the runners and made it to the opposite goal line first. When he started back, the seniors and juniors all thought, *What's going on? This little kid—this skinny, big-eared seventh grader—is faster than us.* They all ran their fastest, and the ten one hundreds went by quickly. Somehow Hillary beat them all.

Andrew said, "OK, guys. OK. Come on over here. We know being in shape is important, and Lord knows you can't win a football game if you aren't in shape, but we have a little problem, because this seventh grader—a boy twelve years old, a boy who barely weighs eighty-five pounds—beat every one of you, so give me ten more."

Once again they were gone. They all ran another two-thirds of a mile. Andrew and Nate were anxious to see who their best players would be.

Clipboard in hand, Andrew wrote down the names of the players from last year and in a separate column listed the new ones. Next he separated the backs and quarterback into one group, then the ends, guards, and tackles in another. Andrew took charge of the backs, and Nate took the ends and linemen, and the boys started their drills—their first lesson on football basics. With thirty-five boys, Andrew knew he had to cut three from the team to get down to his thirty-two-man limit.

The two hours passed quickly, and toward the end of the practice, Andrew said, "Let's run a little scrimmage. Nate, you coach the defense. I'll take offense."

Andrew picked eleven boys for defense and eleven for offense and shouted to the defense, "You boys go with Nate, and I'll take the offense." The rest of the boys took to the sideline.

Hillary watched and followed Nate's instructions. "Boy, when there's a loose ball, when I tell you, go get it."

Andrew ordered a thirty-two fly right. That's where the three back—fullback—goes through the two hole on the right side of the line and then runs long for a pass.

"Hut one, hut two, hut three!"

The quarterback took the snap. There was a pretty aggressive rush—more than what one usually might see on the first day of practice. The quarterback at midfield threw the pass. The fullback was down by the goal line, but the ball fell short by fifteen yards and bounced and bounced, end on end, into the end zone.

All the players came back to midfield, and Nate said, "Hillary, go get that ball."

Hillary ran to the end zone and scooped up the football. This was the first time he had held a new football in his hands, and boy, did he like the feel of the leather. It felt very natural to him; he liked the smell of the football too. He placed the fingers of his right hand across the laces, and just like a rich kid with a brand-new bicycle or a brand-new baseball, he was a kid with a brand-new football. The rest of the group was nearly sixty yards away down-field. Hillary wound up and let the ball loose with a perfect spiral that went fifty-five yards.

Andrew whispered to Nate, "Look at that!"

The two coaches exchanged glances; they could tell this kid was something special. They kept their excitement to themselves but knew this kid was something they had never seen before. He was such a fast runner and could throw a ball like you wouldn't believe.

"Boys, this was a good practice," Andrew said. "Let's finish with two laps around the football field and fifty push-ups. Make sure you get plenty of water to drink and get a good night's sleep. Starting Monday we'll have two practices a day for the next four weeks. Then, when school starts, we'll drop back to one practice a day. First game is in six weeks."

After the players left, only Nate, Father Andrew, and Hillary remained. Andrew said, "Son, you've got quite an arm there."

Andrew thought, *This kid is pure heart—even coming from a very poor family and obviously not even wearing shoes his own size.*

After they put the equipment away, the three of them walked back to the church. Andrew gave Hillary two oranges and two bananas and told him, "Good job son." Nate said to his new assistant, "See you Monday, same time."

Father Andrew thanked Nate for his good work and headed back to the church. He saw the time—12 noon. Tired, he got a bite to eat and then retired to his room to read and to write in his journal. He reviewed the day's events. He had a good feeling about the upcoming football season and smiled to himself when he thought about Hillary and the big talent this kid had.

CHAPTER 13

❦

Sunday came and went, and the new week started. Football practice continued with two workouts per day. The boys needed to get in shape, so practice went from 8:00 a.m. to 10:00 a.m., then 4:00 p.m. to 6:00 p.m. They practiced in the late afternoon in an attempt to avoid the hot summer sun of the Deep South, where humidity usually meant perspiring shortly after seven thirty in the morning.

The week passed quickly, and Father Andrew chose his starting offense and defense players. In the back of his mind, he also thought about the upcoming academic year and his new academic post.

On Thursday morning he woke up bright and early, got dressed, ate breakfast, and headed to the field. As he walked, he reviewed the past week's events; in particular he was impressed with Hillary. The boy was still two full years away from high school but was already as good as most of the players on the team. Oversized shoes and all, Father Andrew could see in Hillary a dogged determination and drive.

Nate and Hillary were already at the field setting up the equipment when Father Andrew arrived. Hillary said, "Good morning, Father."

The sisters had been teaching Father Andrew French, so he thought he would try to speak to Hillary in French.

"*Bonjour*, Monsieur Hillary. *Comment allez-vous?*"

The young Cajun boy responded, "*Trés bien, merci. C'est bien sûr une journée agréable à jouer au football et ensuite aller pêche.*" ("Very well, thank you. This is a nice day to play football and then go fishing.")

Father Andrew couldn't imagine how this young boy had learned French. Hillary had a grin on his face, as if he were Charles Boyer. Andrew had to know.

"Where did you learn to speak French?"

"My grandma, Olivia, taught me to speak French. She taught me lots of other things too."

"What else did she teach you?"

Hillary replied, "She taught me to add and subtract. She taught me about literature and a little bit about science."

Father Andrew's interest was piqued. "I'd like to meet your grandma someday."

Nate burst out laughing because he could speak French, and he was somewhat amazed that this young boy could as well as he did.

It was a good practice, and toward the end, they split into two teams—one offense and one defense. Not yet in football pads but wearing helmets and jerseys, most of the players wore cleats, all except Hillary, who wore sneakers.

"We're going to have a little scrimmage," Andrew said. "Hillary's going to be quarterback for a few plays."

Hillary looked at Andrew. "Coach, are you kidding?"

"No sir. I think you're ready."

Half-joking, Andrew concealed a smile with his clipboard and cajoled, "After all, we've been practicing for a whole week."

With the same amount of pride one would feel when volunteering to serve one's country, Hillary confidently replied, "Coach, I'm ready."

The offense huddled with Andrew, who said, "Let's run a few simple plays, starting with a twenty-four runaround." With his head turned toward Hillary, he added, "In case you don't know what that means, the quarterback takes the snap and gives the ball to the two back—who's the right halfback—and he goes through the four hole."

On the first play, the twenty-four runaround, Hillary took the snap and made a perfect handoff. The right halfback shot through the four hole and gained ten yards. Before the next play, Andrew said, "Let's do a twenty-four Q end around. That's where the quarterback takes the snap and fakes it to the right halfback. Then the QB—that's you, Hillary—takes the ball and goes around the end on the opposite side."

Hillary went up behind the center and barked, "Hup one, hup two, hup three." He took the snap, dropped back, faked the hand-off, tucked the football under his arm, and ran around the left side of the line. The fake handoff gave Hillary about a one-second head start. Soon eleven defensive football players were in hot pursuit. The little Cajun speedster made it around the bend and outran the whole bunch—seventy yards for a touchdown.

Nate and the coach looked at each other and shook their heads. As young Hillary hit the end zone, Andrew blew his whistle and said, "OK, boys, enough fun. Let's do two laps around the field and call it a day."

As the boys ran their laps, Andrew and Nate talked. Nate said, "This boy, Hillary, is something special."

Father Andrew agreed with Nate. Practice finished, Andrew pitched in and started to help pick up the equipment, but Nate freed up the coach, saying, "Don't worry, Father. I'll get the boys to help, and we'll get everything buttoned down. Have a good night. See you tomorrow."

On his way back to the church, Andrew thought forward to Sunday, as it would be his first chance to meet the members of the congregation and deliver his first sermon. He meditated as he made his way back to the church and decided on the topic of his upcoming sermon—"Shoes."

CHAPTER 14

T he second Sunday after Father Andrew's arrival came quickly, and as Father Solomon had requested, it was Andrew's turn to give the Mass and to present a passage from the Bible. Then he would give the homily, the interpretation of the passage.

Father Andrew woke up extra early, ate breakfast, and got dressed, this time not in his coach's garb but in his Holy Eucharist vestment. For the first time, he felt as if he were somewhat of a soldier, perhaps a soldier of God, and that he wasn't going into battle but was representing God in a very special way. Briefly thinking back to his meeting with Saint Hilary of Poitiers, he appreciated that he was on a mission and knew there was a distant past about himself that rested in a part of his brain that he could access, but didn't feel the need to do so.

Andrew tried to calm his thoughts as he walked outside the rectory and into the little garden next to his room. It was still early, a quarter past seven in the morning. The church service started at nine o'clock.

In the church's little garden, there were red roses, white and yellow jasmine flowers, and a large Pink Delight butterfly bush. The humid climate of New Orleans, with the faintest of offshore breezes, was magic for the flowers and plants in this garden. Andrew sat on a wooden chair next to a waist-high statue of Mary. Directly across, on the other side of the garden, stood a statue of equal height—St. Joseph. Father Andrew greeted the two. "Good morning, blessed mother, and hello to you, St. Joseph." Andrew closed his eyes and imagined himself before the congregation, and like an athlete readying himself for a game, he reviewed what he would say. He searched for inspiration and felt comforted with the thoughts that came to mind. Eyes still closed, he heard a high-speed buzz that caused him to open his eyes. Inches away he saw two hummingbirds. The two birds began a little dance, and it seemed as if they were old friends and that they frequented this little garden. Perhaps they were drawn to the garden because of its safety, or maybe there was a higher meaning. They briefly did a dance around him and then touched their long beaks to each other as if they were kissing, and off they went.

Father Andrew checked his watch—eight fifteen. Time had flown by. He went back to his room, got his Bible and notes, and headed to the church. Father Solomon and his helpers and the sisters were preparing the altar by arranging the flowers. Several older priests from the surrounding areas were present as well. Because New Orleans was the big city and Sunday was the day of congregation, many of the parishioners had traveled for several hours. Mostly on foot or by horse, a few by car, all were football fans and wanted to see and hear from Holy Cross's new priest and coach.

Whispers were heard as people from all walks of life started to fill the pews. A large black woman dressed very nicely came up to the altar, made the sign of the cross, genuflected, and went up to Father Solomon. He shook her hand and bowed his head. She had some papers under her arm, which proved to be sheet music. She saw Father Andrew and introduced herself. "You must be Father Andrew. I've heard so much about you from Solomon and the sisters. My name is Eunice Claire. Most people call me Miss Claire. I'm the organist, and I also teach freshmen music."

Andrew replied, "Well, Miss Claire, I'm honored to meet you and look forward to working with you once school starts."

She assumed her position and played a few notes to test the readiness of the organ. Twenty minutes later the entire church was full. From front to back, there were thirty pews on each side of the main aisle; each pew could accommodate fifteen to twenty people. On cue the music began—a beautiful chorale.

Father Solomon took his position, and the service started. "Welcome one, welcome all," he began, "for this is the day of our Lord. Today we have a new member of our parish. His name is Father Andrew, and he's also our new football and basketball coach." Everyone clapped, and Father Solomon continued, "Father Andrew also will be our mathematics teacher for freshmen and juniors. To most of you, he will be Father Andrew. To a smaller number who really get to know him, he will be known as 'Coach.' "

The room filled with laughter as Solomon said, "This is a very special service. Father Andrew will be reading from scripture, and then he'll give us the homily. Without further ado, I introduce my friend and colleague, Father Andrew."

The new second-in-command assumed the podium, opened his Bible, and said, "I welcome each and every one of you to our house, the house of the Father, Son, and Holy Spirit. This is a wonderful day, a day we all will celebrate."

He took a moment and surveyed the congregation. There were people from all corners of the city. Whites and blacks and everything in between. In this church it appeared that the lines of color didn't matter the way they did in the rest of this city and, unfortunately, around the country.

In the first pew, Andrew saw a few of the football players he had coached for the last two weeks. He saw people who had been weathered by the Depression, which had started almost nine years ago. Worry was worn into their faces. Several older ladies in their Sunday best with fancy hats were already fanning themselves with paddle-type fans. Father Andrew's eyes fell upon an older man, perhaps age sixty, who had an enormous smile and a large belly and wore a tight vest with buttons that looked ready to pop.

Andrew got the feeling that everyone was on his side. "Thanks to Father Solomon, the sisters, and all of you for welcoming me to your community," he said. "Thanks be to the priests and sisters who have been here before me, and thanks to the Lord for his trust in me."

Andrew decided to update the crowd on Holy Cross sports. "Football practice has started, and I'm happy to report that this year's football team is a good one. Of course, at Holy Cross our athletes also have to do well in school. I'm very pleased that my duties include teaching mathematics to freshmen and juniors. By the way, it looks like our team may be a contender."

The congregation cheered, and everyone clapped. Andrew even heard a few hoots from the ladies fanning themselves. Ice broken, he said, "Please rise, and open your Bibles to Matthew twenty-five, verse thirty-one, and follow as I read from the scripture. 'When the Son of Man comes in his glory, and all the angels with him, then he will sit on his glorious throne. Before him will be gathered all the nations, and he will separate people one from another as a shepherd separates the sheep from the goats. And he will place the sheep on his right, but the goats on the left. Then the King will say to those on his right, "Come, you who are blessed by my Father, inherit the kingdom prepared for you from the foundation of the world. For I was hungry and you gave me food, I was thirsty and you gave me drink, I was a stranger and you welcomed me. I was naked and you clothed me, I was sick and you visited me, I was in prison and you came to me." Then the righteous will answer him, saying, "Lord, when did we see you hungry and feed you, or thirsty and give you drink? And when did we see you a stranger and welcome you, or naked and clothe you? And when did we see you sick or in prison and visit you?" And the King will answer them, "Truly, I say to you, as you did it to one of the least of these my brothers, you did it to me." ' "

Father Andrew finished the reading and allowed for a brief period of silence. "Please be seated."

Several seconds passed as everyone sat down. A few people cleared their throats, while others whispered and a handful said, "Shush."

"The passage we just read talks about goats and sheep and the Day of Judgment," Father Andrew said. "The sheep dutifully treat everyone as if they were treating the good Lord himself, by feeding the hungry, giving drink to the thirsty, and ministering the sick. Goats, on the other hand, learn that action or inaction toward one of Jesus's brothers or 'children' is interpreted as action toward Jesus himself. I ask you to ask yourself, *Am I a goat or a sheep?* If you're a sheep, are you a perfectly virtuous sheep? Can a goat walk a mile in someone else's shoes? I have an announcement to make—all goats today have an official second chance to become sheep."

The crowd laughed. As the laughter was replaced with waiting ears, Andrew continued, "Years ago there was a young boy. He was very smart and was busy doing lots of things. One day his teacher gave an assignment. 'Read *Huckleberry Finn* and write a report about Huck and Jim. You have one week to complete the assignment.' The boy thought, *This is an easy one. Grandma gave me a copy of Huck Finn for Christmas.*

"One day passed, and boy, was it a busy one. Not enough time to read today. Another day passed, and the boy said, 'Oh, man, tomorrow from four to eight, I'm going to read.' Looking for the perfect time, the boy was procrastinating. At four the next day, his friend Gary came over and asked him to play ball. The boy thought about it and decided to join his friend. He promised himself he would wake up at three in the morning the next day to read about Huck, Tom, and Jim. Soon it was near the one-week deadline, and then it was too late to even begin—paralysis had set in.

"Ladies and gentlemen, that little boy was me. In life, perfection can be the dead enemy of good. Try to do a good job at everything you do. Don't wait for the perfect time. Waiting for the perfect time may guarantee the job will never get done. Get started right away with the job. Do a little bit here and there, and settle for a good job. Don't insist on perfection at all costs. Instead of walking a mile in someone's shoes, start with a few steps.

"A hummingbird builds its nest one twig at a time. Those of you who are sheep, try to be good sheep, and try to be a little better each day—baby steps are OK. To those of you who are goats, take one step in another's shoes just two times and see how you feel. Soon one step will be two, then four, then eight, then sixteen. Before you know it, you will be a sheep. Going from goat to sheep will make you a teacher who is now able to give teaching to other goats. You will also be able to identify goats dressed in sheep's clothing. Walk a mile in someone else's shoes, but begin that mile with only a step or two. Goodness comes from good, not from perfection. Try as we might, we are, after all, human beings and not perfect."

Everyone in the church seemed to understand this message, and immediately Father Andrew felt a strong bond with the diverse congregation. For several moments a nearly overwhelming connection occurred—as if the emotions of heartache and triumph flowed from the hearts of these people through his own heart; first the feeling was heavy, then light, as if his heart had the beating wings of a hummingbird. What an honor to have such a feeling.

Father Andrew blessed the congregation and looked toward the organist, who, on cue, began the closing hymn. When the service ended, Andrew and Solomon, along with the three sisters, exited the church and walked down the aisle to the front of the church so they could meet the parishioners.

Father Solomon, Father Andrew, and the sisters shook hands with person after person as they passed; one could tell the congregation had been touched. As the last person left, Father Andrew thanked Father Solomon and the three sisters, and then Father Solomon and the sisters went back to the rectory. Father Andrew, still on the church's front steps, looked up into the sky and took in a deep breath of air. It felt good.

As he turned to return to the rectory, he nearly bumped into a woman who said, "Father, my name is Olivia Olinde. The young man who you've been helping is my grandson, Hillary. I'm very thankful for the help you're giving him, and in appreciation, my mama and I would like to invite you over for dinner as a welcome and thank-you."

Father Andrew usually wouldn't take up such an invitation without knowing a person better, but he saw in this woman's dark-brown eyes a sense of purpose that intrigued him. He said, "Thank you. I'd be honored to dine with you and your mama."

Olivia said, "We live at one twenty-six Rachel Street. It's a small farm, and we'd love to have you for Saturday night dinner next week. Please come at six o'clock, and once again thank you for helping my grandson."

"Thank you, Mrs. Olinde. I look forward to seeing you and your mama next Saturday at six."

At Sunday dinner Father Solomon appeared relieved and happy about how well Father Andrew had been accepted. In celebration of Andrew's sermon, Sister Madeline had made a rum cake. After dinner they enjoyed their cake and drank tea in the great room just off the rectory. Sitting before the big stone fireplace, they became mesmerized by the dancing yellow, orange, and blue flames. Thanks to Father Andrew, the rectory and church were full of a new energy, and all felt a new sense of calm and peace. After Sister Madeline heard Father Andrew's sermon and discourse, she felt a rejuvenated sense of purpose. She also felt a new feeling for Father Andrew—it included admiration with a few extra heartbeats, which wasn't exactly how she felt about Father Solomon. She felt herself blush and thanked God for allowing her to feel extra feelings in this beautiful moment. A loud pop crackled in the fireplace, which startled Madeline. Reflexively she grabbed and squeezed Father Andrew's hand.

Father Andrew, feeling the effects of the rum, decided to take a little walk to get some fresh air. He bid the sisters and Father Solomon good night and exited the great room. Once on Canal Street, he saw the lights of the French Quarter about a mile and a half ahead. This was the most central part of the community, and it had electricity. It was a warm summer night, and a full moon illuminated his path. Andrew took out his new pocket watch, a gift from Father Solomon. He pressed a little button, and the cover popped open; it was eighty twenty.

He liked to hear the *tick, tick, tick* of the watch. He felt a surreal feeling as the *tick, tick, tick* reminded him of *lub dub, lub dub, lub dub, lub dub.*

An insightful feeling overwhelmed him—that the *lub dub, lub dub, lub dub* sounded like the heartbeat of his mother. *How could that be?* he wondered.

He closed the cover of the watch and enjoyed his rum-cake afterglow as he quickened his pace toward the French Quarter. He heard music and loud voices as he entered, and even though it was Sunday, the bars and clubs were open.

He came upon a tavern and saw the patrons spilling out through the open doors and onto the street, laughing and carousing. As he passed, they all stopped. A few saluted him, since they didn't remember how to greet a priest. One of the guys said, "That's Father Andrew. He's the new football coach at Holy Cross."

Upon hearing this news, all the men in the establishment came out onto the street, as if they were seeing the president walk by. They swarmed around Father Andrew and tried to shake his hand. Taken by surprise, Father Andrew realized his new position. As coach he was somewhat of a minor celebrity, so like any good politician running for office, he shook hands and patted them on their backs and offered thanks for their support. Along with offering hope, Andrew added a bit of prognostication. "We have a real good team this year," he said.

As he continued his walk past a few more establishments, he came across a tiny chapel that he recalled Father Solomon mentioning, but it was closed. Next he came up to a corner where he saw two women. Although it was starting to cool down, most people were fully dressed, but these two were somewhat scantily clad. Father Andrew remembered seeing magazine pictures from the Roaring Twenties of so-called speakeasies and immediately put two and two together, believing these women were ladies of the night. As he walked past them, he nodded and said, "Good evening, ladies."

Not used to being given a high level of respect, the two women felt at ease with the priest's friendly way. Since they hadn't seen him on their corner before, they guessed he was new and replied, "Good evening, Father. Welcome to our town."

Father Andrew made a big circle and followed the full orange moon along his little journey and headed toward the Mississippi River, which was several blocks away. Walking toward the "Big Muddy," Andrew heard crickets, frogs, and the chatter of birds. New Orleans was a city under sea level, and close to the river, off to his left, was a little bayou. He peered between the trees and water and saw four little burning campfires and heard people talking and laughing. Down by the docks, he counted fourteen dory fishing boats all tied down and ready for the next day of fishing, which would start at 4:00 a.m. Andrew thought some of the people in the swamp were probably fishermen who were keeping a close watch on their boats. The moon extended its reflection over the muddy river and lit up the entire visible stretch of water. As he looked over the illuminated river, he heard the two-second blast of a horn from a steamer, and around the bend he spotted a passenger steamer heading up to St. Louis.

Andrew watched for several minutes, until the boat was out of sight, but still heard its high-pitched whistle at each turn. He continued his walk, and as he turned to go home, he heard a sound between two of the docked boats. With caution he investigated. It turned out to be the whimper of a little puppy. The dog had black hair, long legs with big floppy feet, and a splash of white on her chest; she came right up to him, as if she had no home.

"Come here, girl."

Father Andrew picked up the little one and thought she was no more than six weeks old. Not exactly sure what kind of dog it was, he said, "You need a home, don't you?" He figured he would take the puppy back to the church until he found her a good home. As soon as he picked her up, she nuzzled her head against his chest, and as he walked back to the church, she started to snore.

Andrew returned to the church with his new friend and wondered what was the best way to tell everyone. He opened up his jacket and thought, *God forgive me*, perhaps he should conceal the puppy as he walked through the front door.

The sisters and Father Solomon were still awake, enjoying the fire in the great room, and as Andrew entered, he greeted everyone; they were glad to see him return home safely.

Father Andrew said, "Well! I think I'm going to turn in a little early tonight. It looks like a busy day tomorrow. It's going to be a—"

Woof, woof.

The three sisters and Father Solomon turned their heads in surprise, but Andrew acted as if nothing were amiss. He tried to conceal the squirming little canine that bulged under his coat, but finally the pooch poked her head free so all could see. The little one squealed and whimpered, so Andrew had to admit the jig was up. He unbuttoned his coat, and the three sisters came up and huddled around him. The puppy jumped into Sister Mary's outstretched arms. Andrew recounted the details of how he had found the dog down by the docks.

Father Solomon said, "It sounds prophetic to me," and that's all the sisters had to hear, as they said, "We'll take care of her." Giggling, off they ran with their new companion. The long day and adventure-filled night ended, and the fathers called it a night.

CHAPTER 15

❦

The next day was Monday, and Father Andrew woke up extra early, at 5:00 a.m. He readied himself for football practice and reviewed the day's events. In particular he took note that there were only two more weeks of twice-a-day football practice, and then school would start. He imagined what it would be like to teach high school mathematics. Father Andrew knew his knowledge of mathematics was strong, so he wasn't worried about the didactic portion of teaching, nor was he particularly worried about the students or his interpersonal skills.

Ready for the day, he gathered his whistle and clipboard and went to the church garden, where he briefly said his prayers and then meditated for twenty minutes. Not even the hummingbirds were up yet. He decided to take a walk to the docks where he had found the puppy. From the east, the sun hadn't yet risen, but there was a faint sign of early light and an ever-so-slight pink tinge to the clouds. Looking west he saw the full moon from the previous night just starting to set. As he arrived at the docks, he saw the dory fishermen bringing in their catch. Traps and nets on board, the fishermen surveyed, sorted, and readied their catches of lobster, crab, mussels, and shrimp, along with salmon and the occasional walleye. These fishermen had dark skin from exposure to the sun, wrinkled faces, and a saltiness about them that only could be found in a Rudyard Kipling book.

Andrew checked his watch and saw the time had slipped by; it was five after seven. He knew Nate and Hillary would be at the football field at seven thirty and that the rest of the boys arrived a few minutes before eight. The boys were always on time, as they didn't want to run an extra five laps around the field. As Andrew walked, he thought about the football team; he reviewed each of the players' strengths and weaknesses. He began to form a real plan for the offensive and defensive aspects to this football team. Hillary was just entering seventh grade and was two full years away from being able to play freshman football. Father Andrew felt this young man was destined for greatness, but only time would tell.

He made it to the field by seven fifteen and figured no one would be there, but as he approached the little building near the center of the field that housed the equipment, he was surprised to see the entire team. The boys were huddled in a circle and weren't quite ready for practice. They seemed to have a single purpose of mind. A few minutes later, Hillary and Nate arrived, walking from separate ends of the field; they reached the field's center at the same time.

Leroy, one of the seniors, was the team captain. He called Nate and Hillary and Andrew to the circle and said, "On behalf of the team, Coach Andrew, we would like to thank you for being our coach. We're honored that you are our coach and will be our teacher. We really enjoyed your sermon yesterday, and the idea of walking a mile in someone else's shoes struck a chord with us." At Leroy's feet was a box. He picked it up and said, "Hillary, you're the youngest member of this team, and we're proud of your courage and how fast you can run. The guys all chipped in. We have a little present for you."

Hillary was surprised by the kindness the boys extended to him, but wasn't used to it. Not having a father around had, in a way, caused him to drift away from accepting warm gestures. Too used to struggling and not having enough, he was caught off guard by this act of kindness. He walked toward Leroy, took the box, and said, "Guys, thank you very much."

Thanking Andrew and Nate as well, he opened the box, and what he saw almost brought tears to his eyes. It was a brand-new pair of sneakers. He took one sneaker out of the box and was awestruck. The shoes had white shoelaces, no scuffmarks, and no holes, and they looked like a perfect fit. Profusely giving thanks, young Hillary sat down, took off his old shoes—which he had gotten from the neighbor's trash—and carefully put the old shoes in the box, as if they were his most prized possession. He quickly laced up his new shoes and stood up with a smile on his face that went from ear to ear.

Father Andrew said to the boys, "Thanks, guys. This really means a lot to me personally." Nate had a few tears in his eyes. Andrew said, "OK, boys, let's start practice a little early. We'll finish our conditioning this week, and next week school starts."

The boys groaned at the notion of school starting and the idea that summer was over. Where had it gone?

Practice started, and Andrew blew his whistle, "OK, let's warm up. Let's do ten one hundreds and fifty pushups."

Another blow of the whistle, and the boys were off.

The day's practice went well. Nate noticed Hillary was growing; even though it had only been a few weeks, it seemed he had grown an inch and put on five to seven pounds.

Twice-a-day practices continued, and the week flew by. Friday-afternoon practice ended, and Andrew said, "Boys, have a good weekend. Get plenty of sleep, and be ready for school next week."

The boys headed home, and Andrew and Nate made sure Hillary went in the right direction toward home. Then they finished packing up the equipment and walked back to the church.

Father Andrew said, "Nate, I really appreciate your help. You're a fine man."

Nate said, "Oh, Coach, you don't have to say that. These are my people, and this is what God wants me to do."

"Well said, Nate. God bless you. See you Monday."

When Father Andrew arrived at the church, he entered the garden and had some lemonade with Father Solomon. Andrew recounted the events of the day to Solomon and reminded himself that tomorrow night he was supposed to have dinner with Hillary's grandmother, Olivia, and her mother, Rosa.

Tired from his busy week, after dinner Andrew retired early to his room and hit the hay. Lying in bed, eyes closed, he thought about the past few weeks as well as Solomon, the sisters, and Holy Cross. As he drifted off to sleep, a vision of the angelic smile and sound of giggles from Sister Madeline came to mind.

CHAPTER 16

S aturday was one of Father Andrew's favorite days. There was no football practice, so he had a day to recoup his thoughts from the past week and also gather his thoughts for the upcoming week. The forthcoming Monday was the first day of school, and this Saturday represented the second to last day of summer vacation for students and was the entry weekend into the 1938-'39 Holy Cross High School football season. Father Andrew had readied his mathematics curriculum and reviewed his schedule for the upcoming football and basketball seasons. This would take him through fall, winter, and into the spring.

The day slid by as Andrew meditated, said his prayers, and went for a long walk. The long shadows of the trees outside the church told him it was late afternoon. He was looking forward to dinner at six with Olivia and Rosa. Around five o'clock, he checked the time and wondered where the day had gone. He had to get ready for dinner.

Andrew took a quick shower and changed back into his priestly vestment and clerical collar. Inside his journal he had placed the scrap of paper with Olivia and Rosa's address.

Ah, yes, here it is, he thought. *One twenty-six Rachel Street. I'd better ask Solomon for directions.*

Father Solomon was in the great room listening to his latest record on the Victrola. The crooning voice of Bing Crosby sang "I've Got a Pocketful of Dreams."

Solomon said, "Bing sounds great, doesn't he? Tell me, Andrew… 'A Pocketful of Dreams' might make a good topic for a sermon, don't you think?"

Andrew said, "Sure would, Solomon." Once Bing finished his song, he asked, "How can I get to one twenty-six Rachel Street?"

Having known Olivia and Rosa for several years, Solomon knew they lived on a farm a couple miles out of town. "The Ninth Ward stretches from the Mississippi River all the way up to Lake Pontchartrain," he said. "The Olindes live just off the road about halfway between here and Lake Pontchartrain. You'd better take the car."

Caught by surprise, Father Andrew said, "Car?"

"You know how to drive, don't you?"

"Of course I do."

Sister Margaret had prepared a gift basket for Andrew to give to Olivia and Rosa. On the outside of the picnic-type basket was a small bouquet of flowers, and inside were apples, oranges, fresh squash, radishes, and a chocolate cake. Father Andrew thanked Sister Margaret for her thoughtfulness.

Solomon said, "I'll fire up the car and meet you out front. Here's a little map." A few minutes later, in front of the rectory, Solomon pulled up in a Model T. Andrew recognized the Ford model. A subconscious memory allowed only one word—"antique"—into his conscious mind. "She's a real beauty, Solomon," he said.

Hat in hand, Father Andrew felt a little nervous venturing out into bayou country.

Solomon said, "This little baby gets us around. Of course it's no Studebaker. It's not an Oldsmobile—it's a Ford, one that Henry Ford himself built."

With headlights on for safety, Solomon reviewed the map with Andrew. "I don't think you can get lost on this one, son. Just follow the winding road. Whatever you do, don't get out of the car, because you'll be going through a little bit of bayou, where there are gators. Gators won't harm you if you don't bother them. You'll be going about twelve miles an hour, so it'll take you about eighteen minutes to get there."

Father Andrew thanked Solomon and got into the car. Happy he remembered how to use a clutch, he put the car into first gear, turned it around, and headed toward the lake. It was a nice drive. The rhythmic sound of the engine, along with the early signs of evening, made for a medley of sight, sound, and smell. Most of the drive was through bayou country. Century-old oak trees with long branches reached high over the road and created shadows that almost came alive.

Andrew made it to his destination in twenty minutes. He turned right and drove down a short dirt road that led him right to the farmhouse. He got out of the car, stretched, and took in the sights.

Before him was a true working farm with both corn and peanuts planted. The sun was starting to get low, and the different colors in the sky were beautiful: pinks and orange and a little bit of gray. There were a few clouds but no sign of rain. Andrew gathered the flowers and gift basket and walked up a little path with marigolds lining each side. The farmhouse looked like a one-room building and showed signs of age, from both wind, and rain. Reaching the house, he walked up three wooden plank steps to a porch. To the right were three rocking chairs.

As he got ready to knock, the door opened, and Olivia Olinde said, "Father Andrew, we're so glad to have you here. Come right in."

Andrew entered the little one-room house. Immediately to the left in the corner was a single bed against the wall that faced a roaring fireplace on the other side of the room. Next to the bed was a nightstand with an unlit kerosene lamp. Under the lamp was a white lace doily. On the other side of the nightstand was another single bed. On the far side of the room, by the fireplace, there was a nice sitting area. The hearth area was the focal point of the room with its giant wood-burning fireplace. Flames were dancing, and the wood crackled in the fireplace, which also served as the oven. The light from the fireplace helped illuminate the whole room.

As Andrew walked across the wooden floor, he heard a creaking with each step and even thought he heard some creatures scampering underneath. At the back of the house was the kitchen, along with a large table with two kerosene lamps, one on each end. Rosa was preparing dinner.

Olivia said, "Mama, I'd like to introduce you to Father Andrew. He's the new priest at Holy Cross who's been helping your great-grandson. Father, this is my mama, Rosa Olinde."

Rosa looked like she must have been close to ninety years old.

Andrew stood within arm's reach and saw the lines on Rosa's face. Along with her gray hair, the years of wear and heartache in her eyes revealed a look that was all too common in the post-Depression era. He extended his hand and said, "Madam, I'm so glad to meet you."

Reaching back to shake Andrew's hand, Rosa said, "Father, I'm glad to meet you too. Olivia and Hillary have told me so much about you that I feel I know you." A smile appeared across her face, and with a twinge of humor in her voice, she said, "From time to time, Father, I've been a goat, but mostly I think I'm a sheep."

Rosa, Olivia, and Father Andrew all laughed.

Rosa spoke with a Creole accent and was articulate in her choice of words. Her skin was dark, and clearly she was black. Despite having been in New Orleans for just three weeks, Father Andrew already had heard different words used to describe a black person—from "African" to "Negro." The other word that started with "n"—somehow, as soon as he heard it, he knew it was a word of denigration and insult, a word that was ugly.

Rosa was charming and had a freshness that transcended her age. Olivia appeared to be around sixty years old and also had completely gray hair. Both women were neatly coiffed and dressed in nice, simple dresses, and each wore a necklace of white pearls. Since the women were wearing their Sunday best even though it was Saturday, Father Andrew at first thought this night would be a special one for these two women. After a few minutes he changed his thinking; because of the deep soulful natures of these women, he knew the evening would be memorable for him as well.

Olivia invited Andrew to sit down and enjoy the fireplace while they finished making dinner. She spoke with a French accent and had a near-perfect level of articulation. Her skin was, near as Father Andrew could figure, Creole—part black and part white.

Olivia and Rosa finished their preparations, and Olivia proudly said, "Dinner is served, Father." They all went to the kitchen prep table, which had been turned into a dining table with the addition of a beautiful tablecloth. It was blue with white lace with two lit candles; Andrew's eyes started to well up as he felt the empathy, suffering, and pride these two women exuded. The food smelled delicious. Olivia brought three plates to the table. Next she added three bowls and a spoon and a fork for each. Rosa served three glasses of water.

They all sat down, and Rosa said, "Father, would you be so kind to say grace?"

"Dear Lord, thank you for this wonderful meal," Father Andrew said. "Thank you for the company of Rosa and Olivia, and thank you for allowing me to be a priest, coach, and teacher to young people. Thank you for allowing me to meet Hillary."

They all said, "Amen," and began dinner.

The three dined on rice, mussels, clams, and shrimp with a spicy sauce. On each plate was fresh okra and a piece of catfish that tasted very fresh. Homemade bread topped off the feast. The three enjoyed their meals and one another's company. Olivia served Sister Margaret's chocolate cake for dessert.

Father Andrew helped clear the table. Then Rosa and Olivia washed the dishes and put everything away.

Rosa asked, "Father, would you like to sit out on the porch?"

"That would be nice," he replied.

The three went out to the porch and sat on the rocking chairs. Father Andrew and Olivia each carried one of the kerosene lamps. It was a warm summer night. The crickets chirped and the frogs croaked; even a few fireflies danced through the night sky. The full moon had completely disappeared, and it was so dark that the twinkling stars lit up the sky. Olivia brought out three glasses of lemonade. Father Andrew took a sip and could tell this was more than lemonade; it was lemonade plus moonshine. He liked the taste, however, and the three of them each downed their first glass. Rosa was the first to go for a refill.

Andrew reluctantly accepted a second glass, half-feeling this was the first time he actually had been able to let his hair down and completely relax in the new environment in which he had been thrust. In the back of his mind, he rationalized that since he was on a mission this evening represented fieldwork.

As they sipped their lemonade, Olivia said, "Hillary is my grandson, as you know. I had three boys. The first was born in eighteen ninety-four, the second in eighteen ninety-six, and the third in eighteen ninety-eight. My boys are named Michael, Alfred, and Charles, and my husband was Charles Jacob Chollet. Charles came to New Orleans in eighteen ninety-one. He moved from Switzerland to America in eighteen eighty-seven, graduated from Harvard University, and became a college professor teaching Romance languages. Charles had a thirst for adventure, for sure, coming from Switzerland all the way to America, attending Harvard, and becoming a college professor. Eventually he moved to New Orleans in the Ninth Ward.

"I was born in eighteen seventy-three, and at age twenty, I met Charles at church. We fell in love. Charles, being from Switzerland, wasn't wise to the ways of America and the separation of blacks and whites. He was truly a lover of language and people. My boys were officially baptized as Michael Joseph Olinde, Alfred Leonard Olinde, and Charles Artledge Olinde. We married in nineteen-oh-one when the boys were three, five, and seven years old. We loved each other, and that's when my boys took their daddy's name, Chollet.

"In nineteen-oh-two, my husband left, and it broke my heart, but at the same time I kind of understood. In nineteen-oh-three we heard that Charles was hunting in West Virginia and somehow got shot. He got shot dead." Olivia opened a book she had next to her and took out a few photographs. "Father, here's a picture of Charles at his Harvard graduation in eighteen eighty-seven. And here's one of my three boys just before World War One."

Olivia started to cry as she brought out a folded newspaper clipping. She carefully unfolded the paper and handed it to Father Andrew, who read out loud under the lantern light.

"Professor Chollet met his death by an accidental discharge of his gun while he was out training some young dogs for hunting. No one was with him at the time of the accident, nor did anyone arrive until after he died. It seemed from his position near a fence that a rail had broken under his weight while he was crossing it and that he was thrown violently to the ground, causing his shotgun to discharge. He died from internal hemorrhage.

"He was well loved by all connected with the university and was held in high esteem as an instructor."

Andrew handed the paper back to Olivia, who carefully returned the pictures and article to her book. Clearly Olivia had experienced immense pain in her life. She was mostly good at hiding her feelings, but not this time.

She continued, "As the boys grew older, they all left and went to Cincinnati, but Alfred came back years later, and around nineteen twenty, he married Olga Gossett, and they had three boys. The youngest one was Hillary. After Hillary was born, his papa, Alfred, left and went back to Cincinnati, and poor Olga, a white woman, started scrubbing floors."

Olivia looked at her mama to make sure she was OK and then continued, "Olga didn't really want to acknowledge that I was Hillary's grandmother, but when she fell on hard times, she had to live with us for a while, and my mama, who had this farm, was able to support all of us. That's when I started to teach Hillary.

"One thing Charles did was he told me, 'I'm going to give you a Harvard education.' He taught me to speak French and English. He taught me mathematics. I learned world history. Charles opened many doors for me. One door, however, that he didn't open was the door of acceptance. When the census people knocked on our door every ten years and asked us if we could read or write, both my mama and I told them no, even though this wasn't true."

Olivia explained how she taught Hillary the same things Charles had taught her. "Hillary loves to read," she said, "and he has a passion for numbers that amazes Mama and me. I learned to love life partly from Charles but mostly from my mama." Andrew looked at Rosa, who had been listening in earnest. All the while as she sipped her lemonade and rocked back and forth.

Andrew said, "Rosa, tell me your story."

Rosa looked off to the left, not away from Andrew because she was embarrassed but because that was the way she always turned her head when she was thinking deeply.

She began, "Father, I was born in May of eighteen fifty. At least that's what I was told. I don't remember my mama and papa. At the age of ten, along with eight other black people, I was brought to live on a farm with the Olinde family. One man said we were slaves. At the time I didn't realize I was an orphan. Also, I have no memories before age ten. One day at the farm, I was sitting on the step of a porch looking at pictures in a newspaper because I couldn't read. I heard a voice from behind. 'Young lady, what are you doing?' I looked up and saw a man. I said, 'Mister, I'm just looking at this piece of paper trying to figure out what I'm looking at.' The man said, 'Come on up and sit next to me, and I'll tell you.' It turned out that this man was Michael Olinde from Pointe Coupee, Louisiana. He spoke with a French accent and was the brother of the owner of the farm. This was a very big farm, with many, many acres. Michael was born in eighteen hundred and was fifty years older than me. In eighteen sixty-five, Mr. Abraham Lincoln freed the slaves, and a few months later the War Between the States ended. Father, at the time I was fifteen years old, and that farm and Michael Olinde were all I had.

"Over the years, Michael would read to me and teach me, and when I turned twenty years old, he produced a paper that said my name was Rosa Michael. I asked him, 'What's this paper?' He said, 'Rosa, this is your birth certificate, and since you don't know who your mama and papa are, I'm going to make my first name your last name, and if anyone asks you who your parents are, you just tell them where my parents came from. My mama came from Maine, and my papa came from right here in Pointe Coupee, Louisiana.' "

Rosa relayed the story as if she were an actor playing all the parts. Her eyes danced, and she became animated. Next she told Andrew, "On February nineteenth, eighteen seventy, Michael Olinde, at the age of seventy, married me."

"Michael Olinde," Rosa said, "was a wonderful person. He loved me, I could tell, and he taught me so much. Even after he married me, for three years we loved each other, but we weren't close in the way a man and a woman normally are. Once I became more grown up, we were close, and shortly thereafter we became the proud parents of my baby, Olivia. She was born in October eighteen seventy-three."

After her story, Rosa whispered, "Father, it must be the lemonade that's making me feel a little giddy. This is the first time I've told anyone outside the family that I didn't know who my mama and papa were. Now, many years later, I think I must have been sold as a slave with these other black people. Of course, that wasn't the word we were called back then. Michael Olinde gave me my dignity. He taught me how to speak French, taught me how to farm, and gave me part of his farm. Father, I'm blessed that Olivia married a Harvard professor and that I married Michael. Imagine a slave and the daughter of a slave marrying a Frenchman who was a businessman and a Swiss man who was a Harvard professor."

Andrew could hardly speak as he took one last sip of his lemonade and thanked the women for sharing their experiences. He looked at his pocket watch under the glow of the kerosene lamp; it was eleven o'clock.

"My, how time flies when you're having fun," Rosa said, and Olivia agreed.

Hoping he could stay on the road and avoid the gators, Father Andrew bid the ladies good night. Well satisfied with the wonderful evening, he felt there seemed to be a higher purpose for this woman, Rosa, who didn't even have a last name at one point, a woman who had been a slave but still had maintained her dignity.

He felt the parallels between God and Jesus and Rosa, and now Olivia, and wondered whether Hillary perhaps represented something extra special, perhaps related to why he, Father Andrew, was here.

Andrew fired up the Model T, tipped his hat, said good-bye, and headed back to the church, guided by the sounds of the crickets and frogs.

CHAPTER 17

꧁꧂

The first week of seventh grade started for Hillary. He had a new found purpose and direction since he was part of the football team. Although he was still two years away from being able to play in a high school game, the confidence that had been sent his way and the kindness of the guys on the team made him feel valuable. His thirst for learning had been fueled by the teaching he had received from Olivia, who herself had essentially received a Harvard education. Hillary's mother, Olga, couldn't believe the change in her son. One morning, after Hillary had washed his face and hands, brushed his teeth, and done his chores all before six, she joked, "Are you sure you're my boy, Hillary?"

Holy Cross Middle and High Schools taught boys from grades five to twelve. Part of the Roman Catholic Archdiocese of New Orleans, Holy Cross had the motto "*Crux Spes Unica!*" ("The Cross Is Our Only Hope!"). As Hillary's mentor, Father Andrew kept track of his progress and was pleased to hear from his teachers that he was a hard worker—smart, likable, and quick witted.

The Saturday after the first week of school started with another nice sunny morning but with a red sky. Hillary was glad to have a day off. Noticing the red sky, and having spent time with the dory fishermen, he recalled the old sailors' rhyme "Red sky at morning, sailors take warning. Red sky at night, sailors' delight." Once he was dressed, it would be time for breakfast then chores. Thinking about the day, Hillary imagined having lots of fun with his friend Billy.

Alfred and Leroy, his two older brothers, already had finished their chores and were long gone. Olga, now up for three hours, called her youngest son. "Hillary, come get your breakfast."

Hillary downed a glass of milk, a glass of orange juice, a boiled egg, and two bananas— enough fuel for a growing young man for five hours. "Boy, was that good, Mom. Thanks. You're the greatest," Hillary said, as he walked past his mother and headed to the door toward freedom.

"Hold on there, young man. What about your chores?"

Caught, he actually felt sorry for his mother, who worked seven days a week scrubbing floors just to keep a roof over their heads. "I'll help you, Mom. What can I do?"

"That's better. I want you to sweep the walk, bring some fresh water from the well, and bring in some wood for the stove and fireplace."

They lived in a two-room house—essentially not much more than a shack—with no electricity and no running water. The house was located in the Ninth Ward close to Holy Cross.

After finishing his chores, Hillary said, "Good-bye, Mama," and ran up and hugged and kissed her.

Sort of taken back, Olga told him, "Be careful, boy. Don't go by the docks, and be home by dark."

Nearly at full speed, Hillary briefly turned back and replied, "OK, Mama."

Billy's house was a big four-room home with electricity and running water. His dad was a businessman in the French Quarter, but Hillary didn't know exactly what he did. He knew his buddy was Jewish and went to a different church. Billy's dad knew that Holy Cross teachers were good and his son wanted to play football, so it was an easy decision to choose Holy Cross as his school.

Hillary ran to Billy's house, and in about twelve minutes, he covered the two miles. His teammate was an incoming freshman at Holy Cross and was also on the football team. Since they'd known each other since early childhood, Billy was like a brother to Hillary; they were best friends.

The boys had a lot of fun that day. First they went to the Mississippi River and fished. They each caught two catfish and brought the fish with whiskers back to Billy's house and gave them to his mother.

Happy to receive the gift, she said, "Thank you, boys. I'm going to save these for dinner tomorrow. Hillary, would you like to have dinner with us tomorrow night?"

Hillary answered, "Thanks, Mrs. Moskowitz. I sure would, but I'll have to check with my mom."

After delivering their catch, Billy and Hillary ran into seven of their friends, who ranged in age from nine to thirteen years old. All boys, they decided to play stickball. Akin to baseball but requiring less equipment, it was ideally suited for poor kids. They used a broomstick without the bristles and created a ball with a N'awlins twist. Instead of using an old tennis ball, the boys used a small wooden ball wrapped with rubber bands then with layers of wet newspaper. The result was a ball that, when hit, made a sound close to the *thwack* heard when the college boys played baseball and hit a fastball on the sweet spot of the bat.

All the youngsters had desires to attend LSU or Tulane, and play football, baseball, or basketball. Splitting into two teams, one Holy Cross High and the other Jesuit High, for several hours the boys were big league players. The older ones gave the younger ones a chance, and they all had a good time. The final score was thirty-two to thirty-one, with Holy Cross edging out its rival.

Following the game, Hillary and Billy went back to the river and couldn't believe it was late afternoon already. With no sign of "red sky at night," the two friends watched the sun start to set over the old river. Almost as if there were a clock inside their stomachs, they knew it was time to go home for dinner.

Since it was Saturday, the boys wanted to have a little night-time fun. So they stopped off at Hillary's house, and told his mother they were going to have dinner at Billy's. Then they went to Billy's house, and told his mother they were going to have dinner at Hillary's. Off the hook and not having to report home early,

Billy said, "Hillary, my daddy has a restaurant and business in the French Quarter. Let's go see it."

Hillary thought this wasn't exactly an excellent idea, but Billy was two years older and in high school, so Hillary figured it would be OK. From Billy's house, taking a straight-line route, it was about two-and-a-half miles to the French Quarter.

The two decided to take the scenic route along the river. Walking toward town and the French Quarter, they could smell both the ocean and the river. There were trees on the northern side of the river, and as they walked along a little road, they saw boats of all kinds travel up and down the river. Mesmerized by the sounds, smells, and sights before them, they wondered what their futures would be.

Hillary, in particular, had heard Grandma Olivia tell him the Olinde family went all the way back to the 1700s, and that all of them had lived in the Pointe Coupee Ninth Ward region. Hillary wondered whether he might wind up living his whole life in the Ninth Ward. It didn't sound too bad, but he also believed things might be different for him.

The two took their time, spoke to a few friends they ran into, and skipped stones into the Mississippi; they hoped to bounce one all the way across to the other side, but it was just too far. Around seven thirty it was just starting to get really dark as they arrived at the edge of the French Quarter.

Billy said, "My daddy's business is just a couple of blocks away."

For Hillary the excitement started to build. Hardly ever venturing into the French Quarter, but hearing stories from the older boys, he grew cautious but still wanted to see as much as possible. They walked past different businesses, many of which were bars. Even at this early-evening hour, there were already signs of people who had been drinking too much. The two young men especially liked seeing all the different modes of transportation—cars, bicycles, horse-drawn wagons—going up and down Canal Street. The latest models of cars were evident, and they even saw an occasional Model T Ford.

Pointing to one, Hillary said, "That's what Father Solomon and Father Andrew drive."

Laughing, Billy said, "Hill, I may sound like an abercrombie (slang for "know-it-all"), but that Model T is all wet. I'm going to get me a snazzy car."

The boys walked past the Saenger Theatre, which was playing *The Adventures of Robin Hood,* starring Errol Flynn. Both wanted to go to the movie but knew it would cost a dime, and upon realizing they actually didn't even have five cents between them, Billy said, "I'll show you my daddy's place, and maybe we can get something to eat."

They came to a street corner and turned right. This led down a side street that was basically a dimly lit alley. A bell-shaped streetlight on the main road cast a beam of light on the alley, splitting it partly into light and dark. Hillary and Billy could see their shadows as they walked. As they glanced down at their shadows, suddenly two more shadows appeared. Two strange men in their late twenties stepped into the light. What they saw next sent chills up their spines. They had heard some of the other football players

talk about guys like this, and one time Hillary had seen a similar picture in a magazine. The boys saw two men dressed in zoot
suits—high-waisted, wide-legged, tight-cuffed pleated trouser suits
with long coats with wide lapels and padded shoulders.

These two zoot-suiters also wore felt hats with a feather pointing out, and they both sported French-style shoes. One of the fellows had a long chain with a watch that went from his vest to his
pant pocket.

Having seen some Alfred Hitchcock films, the boys felt a
spine-tingling fear as they walked past these guys. Hillary and Billy
couldn't see the two men's faces, and as they quickly scampered
past, the two zoot-suiters looked right into the eyes of the two boys
but didn't say a word. Finally, reaching the end of the alley, the
pair made a left turn, which led to another alley. Six doors down
was the backdoor entrance for Billy's dad's restaurant. Billy said,
"This is my daddy's business."

They walked through the back door into the kitchen. Hillary
blurted out, "Man, this is huge!" It was a big kitchen with Chinese
cooks preparing all types of dishes—steak, chicken, fish, soup, and
potatoes. The smell of blackened fish, blackened steak, and jam-
balaya, along with the fanfare of waiters carrying big trays in and
out, made it seem like they were cooking a feast for a king. Billy
led Hillary through the kitchen and walked right up to a big black
man named Alfred.

In the deepest voice Hillary had ever heard, Alfred said, "Hello,
Billy, who's your friend?"

Billy replied, "This is my teammate, Hillary. We're both on the football team at Holy Cross High School."

Alfred tried to make the boys feel welcome. "Well, guys, glad to have you here. How's everything going?"

They stood there chitchatting for a while with Alfred; all was well until one of the waiters took a big tray of food through the double swinging doors into the restaurant. Both Hillary and Billy heard loud music and smelled food and cigar smoke. As the doors flung open, they saw dancers wearing basically no clothes on a stage. As if a snake charmer were playing a flute to hypnotize them, the sights mesmerized the two.

Alfred could see that the twelve and fourteen-year-old boys were quite impressed. "Boys, come on over here," he said, and took the young men to the edge of the kitchen, where just off to the right, there was a little window. The peep hole was held closed by a latched wooden door. Alfred unfastened and opened the door, exposing what was behind. Then he proudly announced, "These are the VIP seats."

There was no glass in the window. As if they were sitting at a table in the back of the establishment, the boys were transfixed by the sights before them. Two pairs of eyeballs were glued to the dance stage. The boys were excited and couldn't help smiling.

Of course young men who had older brothers and friends had all been shown certain magazines with certain parts of a woman's anatomy, but Billy and Hillary never had seen this in real life. Hillary remembered one time he had accidentally seen his mama by accident, but these women didn't look like her.

For at least five minutes, the lucky ones watched through the window and saw men smoking cigars, eating and drinking, laughing, and occasionally looking up at the stage, where woman were dancing without any clothes from the waist up.

Finally, Alfred said, "OK! Boys, that's it! That's enough. Any more and you'll go blind." He wiped a tear as he laughed. Regaining his demeanor and putting his arm around Billy, he said with a Creole accent, "Guys, we'll make you a little plate." He told one of the Chinese cooks, "Give them the po' boy special."

Weak-kneed after the girlie show, the now enlightened two were glad to sit down for a few minutes while the cook prepared their dinners. Once the meal was ready, Hillary and Billy sat at the edge of the kitchen and ate Cajun-grilled chicken and fresh baked bread. Because fresh fruit was a rarity, they decided to save it for the warm part of the day tomorrow, and when hot and sweaty, each would cut their oranges in half and suck until there was no juice left.

Finishing their gourmet meals, Hillary and Billy thanked Alfred and left out the same door they had come in through. Retracing their steps down the back alley, the two took a right-hand turn into the other alley that led to the main street. This time, about halfway up, the two zoot-suiters were blocking the alley.

Billy had gone through his growth spurt already. Almost six feet tall and weighing 170 pounds, he was the fullback on the football team, even though he was just a freshman.

The man with the watch rudely barked, "Hey, where do you two think you're going?"

Billy said, "We're going home," and with that the other one pulled out a switchblade and flicked it open to reveal the biggest knife either boy had ever seen.

Pointing the blade first at Billy, then Hillary, the knife-wielding zoot-suiter said, "I could slit your throats right here, right now."

The other one right at Hillary and said, "Give me your shoes."

This was the first pair of brand-new shoes Hillary had ever owned; there was no way he would give up his shoes. Hillary looked at Billy, Billy looked at Hillary, and they both had the same idea—they'd better make a run for it, or else they were going to be in big trouble.

Billy tackled the man with the knife and said, "Hillary, run!"

Hillary darted to the edge of the alley, and seconds later he saw the two zoot-suiters as they ran down the alley, took a left turn, and went out the back way. At the same time, he screamed Billy's name, but Billy was lying on the ground, not moving. Hillary saw two sailors walk by and pleaded, "Can you please help? My friend is hurt."

The two sailors and Hillary ran to Billy, and one of the sailors slipped in a pool of blood that was already forming. They could see Billy was in agonizing pain. He had been stabbed behind the knee, and bright-red blood was squirting out. One of the sailors, having received advanced first-aid training, told Hillary, "Give me your shirt."

Hillary took off his shirt, and the sailor tied it around Billy's thigh and made a knot to stop the bleeding. The sailor said, "We've got to get him to the hospital." They looked right at Hillary and said, "There's a hospital just down the street. We'll take him there. Go and get his mom and dad."

Hillary instinctively said, "OK!" and ran the two-and-a-half miles back to the Ninth Ward. He made it in about twelve minutes, running as fast as he had in his life. He went straight to Billy's house and knocked on the door. No one was home! Not knowing what to do next, he ran to the church and knocked on the door, and Father Andrew answered. It was nearly nine thirty in the evening.

Seeing that Hillary was out of breath and upset, Father Andrew asked, "What's wrong?"

"Billy was stabbed," Hillary said, "and two sailors took him to the hospital in the French Quarter. I can't find Billy's mom or dad."

"I'll get the car and meet you out front."

Father Andrew ran into Sister Madeline and said, "There's been an emergency. One of my players has been stabbed, and I have to go to the hospital. Tell Father Solomon I'll get back when I can."

Andrew pulled the car around to the front of the church. Hillary had been in a car only one other time, jumped in. Off they went to the French Quarter. Gas pedal to the floor, they made it to the hospital in about seven minutes.

The hospital was small, with only about ten beds, an emergency room, and one operating room. Father Andrew opened the emergency room door, and Hillary followed him inside. Within a minute or so, a doctor came out and said he was a surgeon and had examined Billy. He explained that the injury was so severe that he would to have to amputate his leg. The surgeon then told Father Andrew, "I need your help. There's no one else here in this damn hospital except a couple of nurses, and we have to operate right now."

Father Andrew and the doctor wheeled Billy into the operating room. The nurse held a mask over his face, delivering ether, and another nurse was preparing some instruments. Scrubbing at a sink outside the OR, the surgeon told Father Andrew, "This boy is bleeding to death. Don't worry, Father. I'll tell you what to do."

Andrew heard a slur in the surgeon's speech and wondered whether it was a Southern drawl or something else. Hillary accompanied them into the operating room but only as an observer. As they got close to Billy, they saw that blood was starting to gush from behind the knee as Hillary's shirt was starting to come loose. The nurse quickly poured soap then alcohol on the leg then placed cloth drapes around Billy's limp body.

Deciding that the overwhelming smell wasn't the ether, Father Andrew angrily whispered under his breath, "He's drunk." *Drunk as a skunk*, he thought, as he and the surgeon put on surgical gowns. Next they slid their hands into sterile surgical gloves.

Once again the surgeon said, "We have to amputate the boy's leg. There's no hope here." Looking woozy and glassy-eyed a half minute later, the surgeon slurred, "I have to go vomit. I'll be back in a few minutes."

This left Billy, Father Andrew, and the two nurses. With Hillary watching, Father Andrew felt the urgency of trying to help Billy. Perhaps through divine inspiration, Andrew knew something in his subconscious past could help. A calmness overtook Andrew, and with it an awakened instinct and memory. He said, "Give me a scalpel."

Not wanting to be insubordinate to a priest, the scrub nurse handed him the knife. Father Andrew made an incision on Billy's left leg from just above the knee to well below the knee on the inside part of the leg, as if he had done this a hundred times before.

Father Andrew told the scrub nurse, "Give me a scissors and forceps."

After seeing the incision the priest had made, the nurse wondered whether he was crazy. She said, "That's not the incision for amputation."

Smiling, Father Andrew replied, "We're not going to amputate."

Scissors and forceps in hand, Andrew dissected deeper, deeper, and deeper. "Give me a Weitlaner self-spreading retractor," he ordered as he picked up the pace.

He placed the retractor between the muscles, and as if he were practicing magic, he went right down to the blood vessel that was causing the blood loss, placed his finger over the damaged artery, and stopped the bleeding. He told the nurse, "Give me a three-o silk stitch on a curved non-cutting needle."

Using his left hand Andrew took the curved needle and needle holder, and placed two perfect figure-eight stitches under his finger, which itself was directly on top of the damaged artery.

Hillary was amazed by Father Andrew, *his coach* and his soon-to-be math teacher.

Father Andrew finished repairing the artery. Then he washed the incision and wounds with sterile water and closed up with a deep layer of catgut and some more silk for the skin. The surgeon came back and said, "OK! I feel better. Let's amputate this boy's leg."

Andrew said, "This boy's leg is fine. There will be no need for amputation."

The surgeon saw the stitches on Billy's skin.

Meanwhile Father Andrew felt the pulse on Billy's foot—the dorsalis pedis artery—and on the inside part of the ankle and the posterior tibial artery.

Andrew announced, "The pulses are fine," and in a slightly out-of-character voice, he strongly broadcast for all to hear, "This boy's leg is saved." He then dressed the leg with a gauze dressing and a loose wrap.

The drunken surgeon got the message, turned around, and left. The scrub nurse felt she had experienced a true miracle. Billy woke up and was taken to recovery in stable condition.

After the operation, Hillary walked up to Father Andrew and said, "Bless me Father, for I have sinned."

Andrew looked at him and asked, "What are you saying, son?"

"I need your forgiveness, Father. What Billy and I were doing is why God made this happen."

Father Andrew questioned, "What were you two doing?"

Nearly crying and feeling guilty as sin, Hillary lamented, "We were at Billy's daddy's business, and we were in the kitchen, and Alfred was giving us a piece of chicken and bread, and we looked through the little window at the ladies' boobies."

Father Andrew smiled, and having received a balanced education himself, said, "God didn't make that happen, and you boys don't have anything to worry about. That's not why this happened."

Hillary felt relieved, as if a weight had been lifted from his shoulders. At the same time, he was so impressed with the keen job Father Andrew had done that at that very moment he decided one way or another he would become a doctor. "Father, you are truly a pip!" he exclaimed.

Shortly after the operation ended, Billy's mom and dad arrived. Words couldn't describe how grateful they were to Father Andrew. Being Jewish, Billy's dad was under additional pressure, as he had just received word that Hitler and his forces were snatching his people and relatives off the streets. Mr. Moskowitz broke down in front of Father Andrew, saying, "I couldn't bear to lose my son."

The next day, Billy told Hillary he was glad to be alive and could barely believe Hillary's description of the operation and Father Andrew's heroic deed. Up and about just two days later, Billy was out of the hospital by the Wednesday after that horrible night. The newspaper headline the Monday after the incident read, "Zoot Suit Attack Saturday Night."

With the aid of a cane from his grandpa, Billy was able to walk and felt well enough to go back to school the following Monday.

CHAPTER 18

⚬〰〰〰⚬

D uring the first game week, Father Andrew was very busy. Having started school, teaching math to freshmen and juniors, and coaching football along with performing his ecclesiastical responsibilities, he was enjoying his new life. The boys and Nate and the coach were readying themselves for the upcoming game on Saturday, which was their home opener. Saturday came, and the game started at noon. It was a nice warm day in the Ninth Ward of New Orleans, and the stadium was packed with at least ten thousand people. Holy Cross won the game eighteen to fourteen; Andrew and Nate felt excited and relieved over the outcome. At the end of the game, the Holy Cross players congratulated their cross-town rivals, Jesuit High, and all the players lined up and shook hands. Hillary wore a Holy Cross jersey with the number twenty-two and felt excited to be included.

The team and community felt a new admiration for the coach. The news about what he had done for Billy had spread throughout the school, the surrounding area, and even the entire region, and the coach started to take a heightened place in everyone's minds and hearts.

At the end of the game, with the help of a cane, Billy also walked through the line wearing his game jersey. After the festivities, Billy's dad came up and shook the coach's hand and once again thanked him for having saved his son's life.

Father Andrew asked Billy and his dad if they could come by the church tomorrow around two o'clock so he could check his incision and maybe remove some of his stitches. Mr. Moskowitz answered, "Of course, Father. We'll be there at two sharp."

After a long day of football, Father Andrew went home, took a hot bath, had a bowl of soup, and went right to sleep after saying his prayers.

The next day was Sunday, and Father Solomon led the way, giving the Mass and homily. At the end, as they always did, Father Solomon and Father Andrew and the three sisters stood outside the church and shook the hands of the parishioners as they exited. This time everyone seemed extra animated and respectful of Father Andrew in particular. Andrew felt proud and also humbled by the outpouring of warmth and admiration; Sunday church events finished around noon.

While eating lunch, Solomon posed a question to the sisters and Andrew. "How would you all like to go fishing? Come to think of it, how about inviting Hillary and Billy after Andrew checks Billy's leg?"

Father Andrew replied, "Solomon, that's a great idea."

Sister Mary, glad too, chimed in, "We love fishing."

The sisters went off to get ready and to make sure that their new puppy, Whitney, was ready to go fishing too.

At two o'clock the rectory doorbell rang, and Father Andrew answered the door and welcomed Hillary, Billy, and Billy's dad, Jacob.

"Come on in, guys," Father Andrew said, "and make yourselves comfortable. Thanks for coming." After exchanging niceties, Father Andrew asked Billy's dad, "Mr. Moskowitz, after we check Billy's wound, how about Hillary and Billy come fishing with Father Solomon, the three sisters, and me?"

Still a bit protective of Billy after nearly losing him, Jacob thought for a bit and then replied, "Sounds like a great idea. I'd love to come myself, but I have to get back to the restaurant and work."

Hearing the word "restaurant," Hillary felt his face turn beet red, and Father Solomon asked him, "Is something wrong?"

Reminded of that night in the French Quarter with Alfred in the kitchen and those "ladies," Hillary answered, "No, Father. I guess I'm just a little excited."

They all moved to the big room, the one with the fireplace, and Billy pulled up his pants leg to above the knee. Andrew removed the gauze dressing, which was held in place with tape, and upon inspecting his handiwork, exclaimed, "The incision looks perfect, but I think we should leave the stitches in for another week." After redressing his handiwork, Andrew felt for the pulses in order to check the circulation. After feeling the pulse on top of the foot, then the one by the ankle, he proudly stated, "Ah, yes, everything is OK."

Father Andrew showed Billy and his dad how to feel for pulses and gave them some good news. "I think Billy will be ready for basketball season, which is just a few months away."

Mr. Moskowitz shook Andrew's hand and once again thanked the coach. "Father," he added, "he's our only child."

Father Andrew said, "After fishing we'll come home and grill our catch and eat just like they did in the olden days."

Solomon chimed in, "Jacob, I'll take the boys home after dinner."

Usually Hillary and Billy could get home on their own, but since Billy was recovering from major surgery, his parents had decided he would be taken from place to place for the near future.

Father Solomon fired up the four-door Model T and brought it out front. Sister Madeline asked Father Solomon if she could drive.

Solomon agreed and jokingly said, "Andrew, why don't you and Whitney sit in the front seat and be our spiritual guides?"

Everyone laughed.

The three sisters, Solomon, Andrew, the two boys, and the latest addition to the church—Whitney the water dog—all climbed into the car, which was loaded with fishing gear. Also on board and carefully guarded by Sister Mary was a soup can filled with night crawlers. North of the Mississippi and still in the Ninth Ward, they headed to Lake Pontchartrain.

Once there they found a little shaded picnic area the city had set up for people to enjoy. It was only about twenty yards from a dock that extended out onto the lake another seventy-five yards. Poles in hand and worms on their hooks, the fishermen and fisher ladies headed onto the dock, which was made from railroad ties. At its end, there were three benches facing north, west, and east. Since they were the only ones fishing, there was ample seating for all. Solomon offered some wisdom—"Fishing calls for patience."

Growing up on the Mississippi, the two boys of course loved the hook-and-worm pastime. All the while they whispered so that the fish wouldn't get scared. After ten minutes, Sister Madeline got a bite. Excited, she squealed as she reeled in a six-pound catfish. Whitney smacked her lips, making it clear she wanted to eat dinner *now*.

Solomon said, "Sister, that is one nice fish."

He helped her take it off the hook and deposited the ten-inch catfish into a satchel used to carry the day's catch. Sister Madeline glanced at Father Andrew from the corner of her eye as she threw her line back in the water, and as she looked at him, she felt a strong admiration and a sense of love, but it wasn't like the love she felt for the other sisters or for Father Solomon. This confused her a bit, as she also had an ache in her heart, and although it made her stomach churn, there was something about these feelings that made her feel more complete.

Father Andrew didn't really notice Sister Madeline in any special way, although he did think she was a very good sister and was both smart and pretty. He knew what feelings of the heart were, including those that extended beyond the feelings of love for God and for your family. His romantic feelings of love, however, seemed to be locked in his past.

Perhaps unintentionally he returned Sister Madeline's admiring glances with his own daydreaming look. Suddenly his inattention was jarred when his fishing pole almost jumped out of his hands.

Hillary shouted, "Holy smoke, Coach. I think you got a big one."

Pole firmly grasped, Andrew started to reel in the big one. He pulled the pole toward himself, reeled, relaxed for a bit, and then exclaimed, "Ouch—this is tough!"

Sweat poured down Andrew's face. Sister Mary offered some help by wiping his perspiring brow, and everyone laughed. As the big one came closer to the surface and popped out of the water, everyone laughed again. It was an old boot filled with water. Andrew reeled in the boot, and once it was on dry land, he poured the water out, along with a little baby catfish no more than three inches long.

He picked up the whiskerless fish and exclaimed, "Look, I caught one—but this little guy is too small," so he threw it back. As Father Andrew was getting ready to throw his line back in, he remarked, "Boy, I sure love fishing."

Everyone laughed, but then Hillary pulled one from left field. "Coach, what is love?" he asked.

Andrew almost dropped his fishing pole but figured he should answer the young man. "Hillary," he said, "There are different types of love. There is love of country; love of your football team;

love for your family; love for God, your creator; love for your mom and dad and brothers and sisters."

Hillary said, "But at our house it's just my mama and my two brothers and me. My daddy left us. Did my daddy love my mama?"

Father Andrew knew this was a difficult topic. He thought back to his dinner with Olivia and Rosa before answering. "Son, we're not exactly sure what God's plan is for all of us. I can tell you for certain that your mama loves you, your grandma loves you, and your great-grandma loves you." He then said, "Hillary, Billy probably saved your life that night. That is friendship, and that is love."

The fatherless boy with hope asked, "Well, Coach, what could bring my daddy back? What makes the love between a man and a woman strong?"

Father Andrew thought about that and noticed he had gotten the interest of the three sisters, especially Madeline. "Well, that sort of love goes beyond the boundary of my being a priest, but my sense of romantic love between a man and a woman and what mates should give each other reflects the same things God gives and expects of us all. Just as God promises never to leave us, so should husbands and wives promise that they will never leave each other. Men should live to please their women just as we should live to please God."

Sister Madeline felt her heart melt instantly and realized that Father Andrew had an inspired wisdom that was extra special. Even Solomon was amazed at Andrew's wisdom and clarity.

After they caught a few more fish, they decided to call it a day, loaded up the car, and got ready to go home. Just as they were getting into the car, suddenly Whitney could no longer stand it. She jumped out of Sister Margaret's arms and ran back to the lake, jumped in, and started to swim. The entire group headed back to the shore and called for her. After three or four minutes of swimming and dunking her head underwater, the wet pooch came ashore, tail wagging and confirming that *everyone* had had a good time at the lake.

The group arrived at the church around five o'clock. Father Solomon took the two boys and their catch and went out back, skinned and gutted the fish with whiskers. Andrew readied the wood-burning grill, then Solomon, Hillary, and Billy grilled the fish. The sisters made a delicious spicy mushroom sauce that they poured over the catfish. Side dishes included fresh collard greens and boiled potatoes.

Father Andrew waited until everyone was seated and said, "Tonight, we have two special guests, Billy and Hillary. Billy, would you like to say the prayer before dinner?"

Billy said, "Yes, Father, but as you know I'm Jewish."

Father Andrew said, "We all worship the same God."

Billy said, "Dear Lord, thank you for the blessing of this food. Thank you for allowing the coach to save my life. Thank you for making promises to Abraham, and please bless all of us at this table."

After the prayer, one and all enjoyed their fresh-caught fish dinner. Father Andrew was impressed with both Hillary and Billy. On the one hand, Hillary was from a very poor family. His grand-ma was the daughter of a slave, yet the values and pride handed down extolled a richness not often seen. Billy, too, had a heritage, courage, and faith that foretold a good future.

Not unnoticed was the worldwide terror of Adolph Hitler. Outside of the United States, Hitler was creating horrible circumstances for the Jews. Andrew remembered earlier in the week when he had read headlines such as "Jews to Lose all Property," "Hitler Tells Mussolini of Colonist Ambitions," "Jews Denied from Czechoslovakia," and "Hitler to Rid Berlin of Every Jew."

Andrew felt empathy for the circumstances of both Hillary and Billy and saw both boys' vulnerabilities and strengths. He again saw something in young Hillary that was very special.

After dinner they all went into the great room, and Sister Madeline brought in a surprise, a chocolate cake. Once the delicious dessert was finished, Father Andrew said to the boys, "I want to show you something that will help you throughout life. It's called 'quiet eyes,' and it can be started by taking the thumb and index finger of one hand and squeezing the little 'snuffbox' in the webbed space on the top of your other hand." He showed the boys the move. "Press in this little space until it hurts just a little bit, hold it for a few seconds, then do it to the other hand. This will relax you and give you a feeling of calm. It'll start off the 'quiet eyes,' which will help you whenever you feel panic or confusion. These 'quiet eyes' will help you access all the knowledge in your brain and assist you in making clear decisions around every turn in life."

The boys practiced their new move and enjoyed the feeling of developing "quiet eyes." Father Andrew then said, "If you practice this 'move' when you're sitting still, it will allow your mind to explore the world of goodness and light. Do not go to the world of darkness. The world of goodness is infinite. That is where love is."

Noting the hour, Solomon said, "OK, boys. It's late. I'm going to take you two home so you can get a good night's sleep before school tomorrow."

Both Hillary and Billy thanked Andrew, Solomon, and the three sisters. The sisters brought Whitney out, and all said good night to Hillary and Billy. The little dog nipped at the boys just a bit with her pointed sharp teeth, and then licked each of them on the hand, as if giving them a kiss good-bye. Solomon first drove Hillary home, then Billy. Back at the church, Andrew took a little walk outside while he waited for Solomon to return.

Thinking about his first month in New Orleans and what he had experienced in such a short time, he felt a nearly overwhelming responsibility for his players, students, and parishioners. He thought, *My goodness! I wonder what the good Lord does, having the weight of the world on his shoulders.*

Feeling less overwhelmed by comparison, Andrew concluded he had a lot on his shoulders but definitely not the weight of whole world. Seeing the lights of the Model T, he waved as Solomon drove the car into the garage. He headed back inside, where he ran into Sister Madeline, who thanked him for a wonderful day of enlightenment. She bowed her head in admiration of Father Andrew. The two said their good-nights, and Father Andrew retired and slept more deeply than he'd ever slept before.

CHAPTER 19

ᏫᏒᎯᎧ

The 1938–'39 football season finished, and Father Andrew was very pleased with his team's overall performance. With a record of seven wins and one loss, they came in first in the city and second in the state championship. Andrew followed Hillary's progress closely in school. Although still in junior high, he proved himself to be a strong asset to the team by working hard.

Young Hillary turned out to be quite the student—an excellent reader and a real wiz at math. After football season, there were two weeks before the start of basketball. Father Andrew looked forward to the upcoming season of "round ball."

After school one day, Hillary went to the gym, where he ran into Father Andrew and Nate; he asked if he could also help out on the basketball team. Father Andrew looked at his assistant coach, who nodded and added, "Practice starts in four days."

Later that day Father Andrew was thinking about the football season that had just finished, including the performance of young Hillary, and thought, *What a kid he is.* Then he remembered back to the dinner with Rosa and Olivia and figured there was a connection between how well Hillary was doing and the help his grandmother had given him.

One day after church, Father Andrew called a meeting with Father Solomon and the three sisters and spoke about an idea he had. Since there seemed to be so many youngsters, both boys and girls, who were growing up without mothers and fathers, perhaps the church could work with the grandmothers in helping these young people gain as good an education as possible.

Father Solomon thought this was a great idea and asked Sister Madeline to work with Father Andrew to develop this program. Father Andrew and Sister Madeline set a time for the following day when they would meet in the garden and talk about his program. The next day, at the meeting, Father Andrew felt excited. First he explained to Sister Madeline his inspiration, which was based on Hillary, Olivia, and Rosa.

Sister Madeline, herself very intuitive and with an enormous heart, understood every word and felt inspired. After listening to him, she said, "Father, let's call this program 'Grandma Knows Best.' "

Father Andrew said, "That's great, Sister Madeline," and then slightly veering off protocol, he told Madeline they would be working very closely and that it was OK for her to call him Andrew. Hearing Andrew's voice, Sister Madeline felt peace, along with a butterfly feeling in her lower chest. They made plans to visit Olivia and Rosa to ask for their help. The goal was to help grandmothers who were raising children, sometimes their own grandchildren, sometimes another person's child or grandchild. The program would offer spiritual and health support from the church and a local medical clinic. Father Andrew and Sister Madeline would teach the grandmothers the best techniques for creating self-sufficient, strong young minds.

A few days later, they jumped into the Model T and drove out to Olivia's farm, through the bayou, this time in the daytime. They heard a few frogs and even saw a few gators scamper across the road. Reaching the little farm, they spotted Rosa and Olivia out in a field that was planted with peanuts and corn—sixteen rows of corn and sixteen rows of peanuts. The corn was ready for harvest.

Andrew and Madeline greeted Rosa and Olivia, and since the grandma and great- grandma had been working all morning, they decided to take a break. Olivia asked Madeline and Father Andrew if they would like some lemonade. Father Andrew remembered the last time he'd had lemonade with Olivia. His eyes opened wide, as if he were about to say something.

Olivia smiled, read his mind, and said, "Father, it's just lemonade."

After enjoying the lemonade, Andrew explained the program and found out that Rosa and Olivia were actually raising three kids whose mother had passed away and whose dad had deserted them. All agreed that Sister Madeline's name was a good one— "Grandma Knows Best." Olivia was put in charge of recruiting other grandmothers, and a class was set to begin in two weeks. The meetings would take place at the church.

Father Andrew and Sister Madeline had developed a curriculum. They announced that the ten-week program would offer classes where the women would learn to develop improved lines of communication with the children they were helping to raise.

Father Andrew said that in two weeks each of the grandmothers would be able to go to the clinic at the hospital in the French Quarter for a checkup. After the stabbing episode with Billy, the administrator of the little hospital had asked Father Andrew to be on the board. As a result, he was able to exact a few perks for his service, one of which was free health care for the grandmothers. At that first class, twenty-five grandmothers showed up.

With Andrew's help, Sister Madeline started teaching the first few classes. Father Andrew saw a real nurturing quality in her that was very special. For an instant he thought back to the times of antiquity; he knew the history of priests and that at one point a priest could marry. Feeling a want for family, he briefly daydreamed about what it would be like to have children and to be with Madeline. Quickly, however, his mind came back to reality as he reflected on his respect and admiration for Madeline, along with the other sisters and Father Solomon.

* * *

Basketball season came before Andrew knew it. Still teaching math to freshmen and juniors, he once again became very busy. Practice took place in the Holy Cross gymnasium, which had been the second place in the city to get electric lights. The first was the French Quarter.

Practice started at three thirty, right after school. Hillary and Nate were working with the equipment when most of the team arrived on the first day; about fifteen boys showed up. Four were returning from the prior year. Three players were seniors, and two were sophomores; one of the sophomores was Hillary's older brother, Leroy. One of the incoming freshmen was his other brother, Alfred. Also reporting for duty was Billy, now recovered from his injury. Father Andrew arrived about five minutes late, blew his whistle, and said, "OK, boys, let's all huddle over here just off the court and talk for a little bit."

He explained what he expected, and although half the kids were football players, he told everyone they would have to earn their positions on the team. Next he started some basketball exercises, including dribbling, running, and shooting from the foul line.

As the boys practiced, Father Andrew looked at Hillary and said, "Son, I want you out here on the court. I want to see what you've got."

Hillary participated in the drills and was once again on cloud nine as he played on the same court as the big boys.

Andrew explained his strategy for offense and defense, emphasized the notion of teamwork, and said, "We only have two weeks to get ready for the season. So, boys, one of the areas where it's important to be good is shooting free throws. It's only one or two points, but that's what can win a game. Let's split into two groups.

Half of you go down to one end of the court, the other half to the other end. Nate, you go with this group. I'll be over here. I want each of you to go to the foul line and take a shot. If you make the shot, you can shoot another one. Keeping shooting until you miss, then it's the next one's turn."

Hillary went with Nate's group, and since he wasn't actually part of the team, he was the last one to shoot. There were eight boys on each side, including Hillary. The first two boys each shot and missed. On the next two shots, one made it and one missed. No one made more than two in a row. When Hillary came to the line, he took the basketball, which almost seemed bigger than him. He shot and made his first free throw. He made another one and another and another and another, until he made seventeen in a row.

This caught the coach's attention, and once again he knew this kid had wells of potential. Alfred and Leroy were surprised to see their little brother practicing with the team. Leroy was the star of the team, which pleased Andrew and Nate, since they now had another Chollet on board.

At first Billy was a little reticent, but before long he had trouble remembering which of his legs was injured. Still evident, however, was his scar, which he proudly exhibited.

Although Andrew knew he had some good talent on the team, he also knew their crosstown rivals, Jesuit High, rarely missed a beat, being well founded in the basics.

* * *

The Christmas and New Year holidays came and went. School started again, and Father Andrew began his sixth month at Holy Cross. The 1938–'39 basketball season was a good one, with the Holy Cross Tigers coming in first place in their league.

Sister Madeline and Father Andrew's Grandma Knows Best program was a big hit. Grandmothers from all around the New Orleans area became empowered, which translated into inter-generational grandchildren growing up in safer, more nurturing environments.

Even the chief of police told Father Andrew, "Since you and Sister Madeline started your program, we're seeing a decrease in crime."

* * *

Rosa Olinde passed away in her sleep on May 5, 1939. Nearly ninety years old at the time of her death, this former slave was finally able to rest. The news spread quickly. Sister Madeline arranged for the wake and funeral. At the time of Rosa's passing, there were nearly one hundred grandmothers in the Grandma Knows Best program. Rosa had been the first one in the program, and her humble ways, along with her community contributions, had made her legendary. At first news of her death, it seemed only a small family service would be needed, but as word spread, people from all walks of life contacted the church and Sister Madeline.

In New Orleans, at that time, a funeral was less of a somber event and more of an opportunity to celebrate a loved one's life. This couldn't have been truer in Rosa's case. Person after person came forward and told Sister Madeline their stories of life with Rosa. More than thirty men and women told her how Rosa had helped raise them when they were young. Each one recounted the loving but firm way she had helped them.

One man, Henri, who was now a banker, said, "She made me do my chores. I didn't have a mama or papa. She loved me and made me feel I was worthwhile. It was her love and support that helped me succeed and have a desire to return the favor." Even the mayor weighed in, making May 9, the day of the funeral, an official day of celebration.

The day started with the Mass of Christian Burial at the church. Father Solomon gave the Mass as Rosa's body rested in a beautiful casket draped with white and red roses. Olivia gave the eulogy, and four of the many individuals raised by Rosa gave testimony as well. The entire church was filled with Rosa's friends and family. After the service the music began; Rosa had a real New Orleans funeral. On that day there was a procession with a French Quarter brass band and drummers who started at the church and proceeded to the Holy Cross cemetery a half mile away. Somber music played as the entire congregation followed. The air was filled with the sounds of "Nearer My God to Thee." Along the route a second line of followers joined in the march. Once they arrived at the cemetery, Father Andrew, Sister Madeline, and Olivia all gave testimony, and Father Solomon gave a final blessing.

After the burial the somber event turned into a boisterous party with upbeat jazz music, as family and friends celebrated Rosa and her life. As "When the Saints Come Marching In" played, the jazz-filled procession made its way back to the church, where everyone enjoyed punch and cookies. At one point Father Solomon was heard saying, "This punch tastes like Catdaddy Spiced Moonshine." Overhearing the comment, Father Andrew remembered his first meeting with Rosa and Olivia and the tasty lemonade they'd served.

CHAPTER 20

❦

The third of August 1940 came, and Father Andrew awoke at five thirty in the morning. The birds were already up for the day and whistled their songs in a pleasing manner. Lying in bed, he remembered this was the weekend of his two-year anniversary in New Orleans. Since it was Saturday and he had the day off, Andrew decided to walk to Lake Pontchartrain. Quickly dressing in shorts and a T-shirt, he washed up and brushed his teeth but decided not to shave.

He walked through the kitchen, where he grabbed an orange and a banana, and then exited the church. Once outside, Andrew began his little trek. Although he had driven to the lake many times, this was his first time on foot. It took about thirty minutes to make it to Rosa and Olivia's farm. Everyone was still sad about Rosa's passing, but as Father Andrew walked by, he could see Olivia and four young people already at work. He waved as he continued his trip to the lake.

Enjoying the walk, Father Andrew was pleased with how well things were going in his life. As he walked around a sharp right turn in the road, he heard a sound just in front of him, and much to his surprise, he found himself six feet away from a four-foot gator. (Being a math teacher he was able to accurately guess its length.) Wondering what he should do, he remembered Father Solomon's previous advice—"Whatever you do, don't get out of the car." Well, he didn't even have a car this time. What was he to do?

Slowly he backed up a few feet, and the gator matched him step for step. Andrew thought he could see the gator smack its chops as it advanced. While considering his options, he heard a loud noise from the bayou and then saw a huge gator emerge from the swamp—this one was twelve to fifteen feet long. The enormous gator made a guttural sound and quickly positioned itself between Father Andrew and the little gator. Saying a prayer, Andrew made the sign of the cross and briefly considered running.

The big one looked at him and then at the little one. Andrew remembered another piece of advice from Father Solomon— "Don't bother them and they won't bother you." He took the advice to heart and stayed still; in a flash the big one turned and pushed the little one into the bayou and followed it back into the swamp. Relieved, Andrew reflected on this frightening event and decided two things—Solomon gives good advice, and sometimes you're better off driving.

Seeing a new theme for a possible sermon, Father Andrew was still trembling and realized he could have been killed. Playing his own devil's advocate, he wondered if he had been eaten, would that have been God's plan? What did it mean when really bad things happened to good people? Was it God's will?

Andrew reconciled this quandary by knowing that God helps those who help themselves and that the best way to help oneself is with the power of the collective consciousness of the human experience. Free will and the ability to make good choices plus this power gives us our best chance to help ourselves. Arriving at the church, Andrew ran into Father Solomon, who asked, "Father, what are you doing up so early?"

Andrew responded, "Good morning, Father. I just wanted to take a little walk and see some nature."

Still a little unnerved by his gator confrontation, he headed into the church and sat in the first pew, went through the Stations of the Cross, and then said a rosary. Afterward he went back to his room and wrote in his journal.

August 3, 1940

Today I almost was eaten by an alligator. Very scared at the time, I realized that my life and the world had flashed before me. Through the grace of God, I survived, but now numerous thoughts and questions are on my mind. Was it free will, or was it God's will that got me first in trouble, then, second, out of trouble? After almost dying, I was glad to be alive. An invigorating strength came over me, and for a few minutes, I felt invincible and kind of selfish. My mind wandered, and my heart did too. Perhaps like a drunken man craving his next drink, I became drunk on surviving and experiencing everything life has to offer. I wondered about love and whether I ever would experience it.

I also lamented about my past and at the same time wondered if my future memories would be ditched into a box in my being and labeled "lamented memories."

How was it that I was able to save Billy's leg? I never thought I could accomplish such a deed—was it me or was it God? My dilemma doesn't seem to be of the heart but rather of the mind. Something in my subconscious is pushing into my consciousness. Is it my nature, or is it the emergence of my demons? It scares me a little, but it also excites me and feels a little like a powerful medicine.

The Carpet

In the great room of our house, there was a carpet. Near the front door, the carpet was stepped on whenever someone came in or went out. As I grew older, the carpet's color started to fade, but somehow it didn't tear and remained strong.

One day I found myself looking at that old carpet, searching for a tag or label. Not finding one, I examined the threads and stitching and looked at the beautiful woven pattern. Years later I still wondered who its creator was. Who was its loom master?

Over the years so much happened

to that carpet. Once it even was splattered with blood. One Saturday, after I had walked on the carpet and was headed to the front yard, a thought came to me. That carpet seemed to have a history and an existence.

What if that carpet represented all the people in the world, humanity as we know it? Who now was the loom master?

God, of course. Imagining this carpet of life, I again looked at the different colors and patterns and became impressed with their interconnectivity. The transformation into beauty occurs when the parts are looked at as a whole. Looking at the threads of humanity, one sees struggle, sadness, hope, and faith. They are all knitted and woven together to create the fabric of society and humanity.

We, not me.
You, not me.
Not me, we.
Not me, you.

—Andrew

CHAPTER 21

෴

Monday, August 5, was the opening of the 1940–'41 football season at Holy Cross High School. Father Andrew felt excited as he readied himself that morning. Also up at 7:00 a.m., the sisters were in the kitchen making breakfast and preparing for a bake sale with the ladies of Grandma Knows Best. They were raising money for one of the grandmothers whose house had caught fire and had burned to the ground. With the money raised, the ladies were going to hold a house-raising party and had plans to build a replacement home.

Sister Madeline saw that Father Andrew was excited and glad to be back coaching football. Trying to conceal their giggles, she smiled, shushed Sisters Mary and Margaret, and said, "Father, I know you're in a hurry, but the sisters and I wanted to tell you we're having gator stew for dinner tonight."

Sister Mary and Sister Margaret burst into laughter, and Sister Madeline almost did too. Sister Madeline reached out and touched Father Andrew's right forearm and said, "Father, we have an army of grandmas out there, and they see everything."

Andrew thanked the sisters for their concern and chuckled to himself. "Sisters," he said, "God bless you, and have a nice day."

Arriving at the field, Andrew met Nate, who was getting the equipment ready. A few minutes later, Hillary arrived, and both Nate and Andrew almost couldn't believe their eyes. Before them stood five-foot-ten and 155-pound Hillary Chollet. Now an incoming freshman at Holy Cross, he was no longer Nate's assistant.

Already aware of Hillary's athletic prowess, Father Andrew was particularly taken by Hillary's demeanor—quiet and soft-spoken most of the time but like a lion when challenged. Hillary was a good student and faithfully came to church every Sunday.

The first few practices allowed Andrew and Nate to scout their talent and see who their best players were. Hillary was fast and tough.

Nate figured, "Coach, I think he should play left halfback on offense and safety on defense."

Andrew agreed, adding, "We can use him on special team plays too. Kickoff returns, punt returns, and special plays where he throws the ball." He couldn't help smile as he reflected back to that first day in the church when he had met Hillary and his mother, Olga. Back then Hillary was a wild skinny kid, and the transformation was remarkable.

Hillary's first football season was a success. As a running back, he gained nearly 9.4 yards per carry—practically a first down every time he touched the ball. He showed proficiency in passing, and on the defensive side, he played safety, expertly making interceptions and running the ball back for big gains. He was an all-around scholar-athlete, and his football prowess was only bested by his basketball abilities.

Times were changing, of course. December 7, 1941, marked the attack on Pearl Harbor. The next day the United States entered World War II. Many men had to leave for war, which created the need for an army of grandmothers to help raise young people. Sister Madeline was busier than ever.

On Dec 17, 1941, Olivia passed away. Again, everyone was saddened. People from the church knew Olivia as a strong "silent" leader and a champion for women's rights and civil rights. In the New Orleans style, everyone celebrated her life and passing with a church service and party.

* * *

Over the next few years, Hillary displayed remarkable development in both basketball and football, along with academic success. Of the many brothers who appeared on the New Orleans prep scene, none left more of a mark than the Chollets. Holy Cross dominated high school sports in the area, primarily because of the Chollet brothers. Besides football and basketball, Hillary played baseball and track. The Holy Cross Tigers won two city and state baseball titles, two city and state basketball championships, two city and state track titles, and two city and one state football championships during those three years. It was clear that the number-one running back in New Orleans was senior Hillary Chollet of Holy Cross. High school flew by for Hillary. Father Andrew looked upon him as a fine wine and wanted to savor every minute of his connection with this young man.

After one basketball game, Hillary came up to Andrew. "Coach, I want to thank you for all the help you've given me," he said. "As you know, my daddy left when I was young, and over the past five years, you've been like a second dad to me. Thanks."

Father Andrew felt touched. "No problem, son. It's been my honor."

As the weeks and months passed, Hillary's athletic skills, along with his easy demeanor, his humble level of interaction, and his quick mind, became legendary in New Orleans. During his senior year, colleges across the country heavily recruited him. The church became his mailing address for all communications.

One Sunday afternoon after church, Hillary came by and met with Father Andrew in the great room of the rectory. They went through the mail and reviewed the college file they had set up. That day they considered Hillary's college options to date. Tulane University had accepted him, and University of Alabama, University of Notre Dame, and the Naval Academy were recruiting him. Just yesterday a letter had come offering an acceptance and a full scholarship at Cornell, an excellent Ivy League school.

Father Andrew said, "Son, you've had quite a high school career, and I'm very proud of you. I know your mama is proud, and

Olivia and Rosa also would be very proud of you. What's on your mind in terms of where you think you want to go?"

"Coach, I'm very thankful for the opportunity you've given me," Hillary said. "It would be wonderful to attend Notre Dame or Cornell, but I'm worried about my mama, so I think I should go somewhere local, either LSU or Tulane."

"You don't need to decide now, but it's nice to have choices."

Later in the week, at around four in the afternoon, there was a knock on the door of the rectory, and two men dressed in suits asked for Father Andrew. The priest greeted the two gentlemen and invited them in. One fellow said he was from Tulane University, and the other said he was a city banker on the Tulane board of trustees. Father Andrew thought these men were there to try to convince Hillary to accept a position to play football and receive a college education. The words that followed were ones he never thought he'd hear.

The representative of Tulane said, "Father, I know Mr. Chollet is quite a football player and that he's been accepted by our institution, but the board of directors has asked me to come and talk to you about rescinding our acceptance. You see, Father, we've found out that Mr. Chollet is not all white, and our institution does not accept an individual whose skin is black or part black. I know you understand this, Father."

Father Andrew, who usually was a person of calmness and moderation (one lady even said he had the patience of Job), felt his ears getting hot and half-wondered whether these gentlemen could see steam coming from them. He had been living in New

Orleans nearly seven years and was known for "walking a mile in another person's shoes." This time, however, he was having trouble seeing eye to eye with these fellows. Despite having empathy for almost everyone, Father Andrew thought, *With these two, it's just not possible.*

The priest admonished the two. "Gentlemen, thanks for coming by, and I don't mind saying you're clearly going to regret this decision. I'm not talking as a priest right now, but I am talking as Hillary Chollet's coach. This young man is the finest athlete New Orleans has ever seen. He can play baseball, track, basketball, and football, and he's smart, engaging, and kind. I would like to thank you gentlemen for coming by, and appreciate the information you've given me. This isn't bad news for us. We will be pushed in a different direction. Now I will talk as a priest and extend my sympathy for your loss. Have a good day, gentlemen."

After the men left, Father Andrew recalled a conversation he'd had with Nate earlier in the day. Nate said he thought something was up with both Tulane and LSU, because his buddy, Clarence Pop Strange, was LSU's football line coach. "Pop told me it had to do with Hillary and his being part black," Nate had said.

Andrew was confused and mad. He felt his blood pressure rise; then suddenly seven-year-old Whitney came up, whimpered a bit, and sat right down on his shoes. She looked up into Andrew's eyes with that "I still love you" dog look that could melt a person's heart.

"Thanks, girl," Andrew said. Whitney got her ears rubbed, and both dog and man felt better. Andrew felt his anger disappear, and a weight was lifted from his shoulders.

The next day Father Andrew ran into Hillary and briefly told him the story of the two men who had come to the church. Not wanting to tell Hillary what to do, he could see the wheels grinding in the young man's head.

Hillary said, "Coach, I'm going to go to Cornell."

"Son, I think that's a very wise decision," Andrew told him.

Hillary said he looked forward to attending Cornell, thanked Andrew, and went home and told his mama. Olga was happy and relieved upon hearing Hillary's news. She hadn't even finished 9th grade, and without help from her husband, she had raised three boys and kept a roof over their heads. Olga was overcome with feelings of relief and gratitude. All three of her boys were going to be college graduates. Her oldest, Leroy, was already at Canisius College in Buffalo, New York, getting an education and playing basketball.

The rest of the school year passed quickly. Hillary sent in his acceptance to Cornell, as well as his letters of decline and thanks to Notre Dame, the Naval Academy, University of Alabama, and ultimately even to Tulane.

CHAPTER 22

⚭

Hillary Chollet, the scholar-athlete, graduated from high school in May 1944 and arrived in Ithaca, New York, in August that same year, ready to start at Cornell University.

While at Cornell, Hillary grew emotionally, spiritually, and physically. Playing both basketball and football and being pre-med, he had a very busy schedule. Hillary, however, had a dogged determination and a drive for success. Every few months he'd write or call Father Andrew to ask questions, seek advice, and update him. Father Andrew was pleased to hear that Hillary attended Our Lady's Chapel at the Newman Oratory on the campus of Cornell University.

The priest presiding was Monsignor Donald M. Cleary. Father Andrew was somewhat familiar with the Newman Centers. Having read many of Father Solomon's books, he knew the Newman Centers were Catholic ministry centers at non-Catholic universities. Originally established through the inspiration of Cardinal John Henry Newman, the centers encouraged and supported Catholic students who were attending secular universities. The very first Newman Club was established in 1818 at Oxford. Cornell University had one of the first US Newman Clubs, organized in 1888. This club eventually matured into a full-fledged campus parish, the Cornell Catholic Community. Father Andrew began writing Monsignor Donald Cleary. After several letters back and forth between the monsignor and Father Andrew, it became apparent that Father Andrew had a special bond with the Cornell sports star, so the monsignor made a few phone calls and saw to it that all of Hillary's sports clippings and information were kept up to date and mailed to Father Andrew and the sisters. One of the letters from the monsignor included an issue of the *Cornell Alumni News* dated April 15, 1948. After dinner Father Andrew called everyone to the great room. Acting a bit like the famous sportscaster Red Barber, Father Andrew, also well known for his storytelling, read the clipping.

"Basketball Roundup"

Captain-elect Hillary A. Chollet, '49, was selected by the Boston Basketball Writers Association as one of the five best players to appear in the Boston Garden. Gale won honorable mention.

Attendance at home basketball games in Barton Hall set a new record of 74,138 paid admissions, an average of 5,703 for thirteen games. The largest paid crowd saw the Columbia game—7,328.

A recent letter from alumni Robert J. Kane, '34, Director of Physical Education and Athletics, pointed to this attendance figure and said, "Basketball has so captured the fancy of all of Ithaca that it now compares in popular favor with football." He paid tribute to all the players on the 1947–'48 squad and singled out two for special mention. Kane wrote:

The basketball players have become heroes to the local kids and the popular favorites of everyone. The spectators are so close to the scene of action in basketball, the players are more readily identifiable than in football or the other sports, and the kids know all the court stars by sight and besiege them for autographs.

This is a development new to Ithaca but one that may have prevailed in times past of which I cannot authoritatively speak. The populace here has always been sport minded but only moderately conscious of the ball players as personalities. This has changed somewhat and most especially with respect to next year's captain, Hillary Chollet. This boy has become the overwhelming athletic favorite of the undergraduates, the townsfolk, the kids, and even the faculty (because he's a top-grade student too). When his name is announced over the loudspeaker in the starting lineup, there is an ovation far more thunderous than all the rest. This is all right with the other ball players because they applaud him too.

Why is this? It is true he has been good all along in football and basketball, but we have had far brighter luminaries in the past, and better scorers even on the ball teams on which he has played. It is clear, however, to us who know him and see him play. He is by all standards one of the most graceful and talented athletes Cornell has ever had; he moves with the superb nimbleness of a panther. But withal he is completely modest, self-effacing, and is above all a team player. He apparently is not concerned with his personal scoring total. He plays to win for the team. His poise, courage, and placid temperament ingratiate him with all, even the basketball officials. Never, at least publicly, has he complained to an official, and this is rare indeed in basketball.

He has two years more of football eligibility, one of basketball. When 1948 football is discussed everyone says, "If Hillary is right, so will be the team." He is a pre-medical student, and with all his athletic activity, he's never quiet. He manages to maintain an 80 percent average.

Feeling like proud mamas and papas, Solomon, Andrew, and the sisters all were delighted with Hillary's progress.

A few weeks later Hillary called the church and told Father Andrew, "Father, Alfred and Leroy are going to move mom up to Buffalo." Leroy was attending Canisius College in Buffalo, where he too was a basketball star.

Halfway through Hillary's stint at Cornell, during football season, Father Andrew and the sisters and Father Solomon got their first television, and the following Sunday, they got a chance to see Hillary and Cornell play against Army at Soldier Field in Chicago.

On Sunday October 24, 1948, Army was heavily favored to win. In the second quarter, Hillary was up for a big run when he got hit from both sides by two of the Army players and injured his ankle. This was after the war; most of Army's players were men who had been through World War II but were home and going back to college. Being grown men, they had a little bit of a size advantage over some of the eighteen-, nineteen-, and twenty-year-old Cornell players. Hillary was carried off the field, and his ankle injury ended his football and basketball seasons that year. It was such big news that Father Andrew even saw a picture of Hillary being carried off the field in *LIFE* magazine. While injured, Hillary poured his attention into his courses and worked on his pre-medical studies.

In March 1949, Father Andrew received a basketball program from the monsignor. In it was an article titled, "Harvard and Hillary." Sitting in the big room at the church after school and basketball practice, Father Andrew read the article. It read, "Harvard had better watch out tonight. The Cambridge Jones are facing a fellow who has raised havoc with them in sports during the course of the last year. He is our captain, Hillary Chollet. Tonight Hillary plays his last game for Cornell homefolks against the visiting Crimson, and if he can duplicate the performance he put on in Syracuse Wednesday, it will be a fitting climax to a sports career."

The program went on to say, "Several days earlier at the Coliseum in Syracuse, New York, Hillary set and broke more records than one could reasonably expect from any individual. A shy, likable guy, Hillary poured in thirty-seven points against Syracuse. He stole the ball from the Orange backcourt and raced down the court to score all by himself. He dropped in nineteen of twenty-three free throws, which indicated Syracuse's strategy in stopping him by fouling, and when he broke the Coliseum scoring record, he received a tremendous ovation from the Syracuse Orange fans. That was another record. The previous fall playing football against Harvard, Hillary scored three touchdowns."

There was more and more documentation of Hillary's football and basketball abilities. Reading another article, Andrew noted a comment from Cornell's legendary coach Lefty James, who said, "Hillary Chollet is the greatest football player I ever coached."

After taking this all in, Father Andrew decided that at tomorrow's church service he would talk about Hillary in the homily. He wasn't exactly sure what he would say, but he knew he would start with a basic idea and then wing it. He had delivered some of his best sermons that way.

The next day, Father Andrew was up with the roosters. Father Solomon was out for the day, working in the soup kitchen downtown, having turned over the day-to-day operations of the church and school to Father Andrew. The service started at nine o'clock with the traditional opening and prayers. Father Andrew stepped up to the pulpit and looked across the congregation. Having been at Holy Cross for some eleven years now, he saw mostly familiar faces but also some new ones. Briefly reflecting to himself, Andrew felt a great deal of satisfaction coaching football and basketball and helping Father Solomon and the sisters, especially Sister Madeline.

Father Andrew began, "It is springtime in New Orleans, and a time of renewal—blooming flowers, baby hummingbirds, butterflies, and baseball. Welcome one and all to the house of the Lord. Today's Bible passage comes from Jeremiah twenty-nine, verses eleven and twelve. 'For I know the plans I have for you, declares the Lord, plans for welfare and not for evil, to give you a future and a hope. Then you will call upon me and come and pray to me, and I will hear you.' "

He continued, "Please be seated. Today I would like to talk about someone you all know, someone who you are all proud of.

As you know, Hillary Chollet is a big football star at Cornell. He's also a big basketball star and one of the finest examples of academia Cornell has ever seen. Hillary wants to be a doctor, and no doubt he will become one. Many of the students at Holy Cross come from poor families, and Hillary was no exception. His mother, Olga, raised three boys with no father. She scrubbed floors so they could have food and clothing. Now you may say that Hillary Chollet was very lucky or that he was given special preference, but I don't think that's the case. You see, I met Hillary when he was just twelve years old. He helped Nate, my assistant football and basketball coach. Of course he did have a lot of ability, but Hillary was humble and had no sense of entitlement. Recently he played in a basketball game against Syracuse. In that game, Syracuse couldn't stop him with one defensive man, so, their strategy was to foul him. As you know, in basketball if you're fouled, you get to take a foul shot. They fouled him twenty-three times. He made nineteen out of twenty-three foul shots, which is a national collegiate record. In life when you are fouled, with patience and hard work, you can turn a foul into a success. The Lord wants you to have a future and hope. Pray to the Lord and then call upon him."

Given Hillary's drive, attitude, and doubling down when the going got tough, at the end, Father Andrew found himself saying that Hillary Chollet was a fine example of a "soldier of God."

As those words came out of Father Andrew's mouth, a light went off in his head, and he realized this young man was the individual Saint Hilary of Poitier had talked to him about. Father Andrew was overwhelmed with emotion. He finished the homily in the usual manner and met everyone outside the church; the entire congregation was touched, proud, and hopeful.

After church, Father Andrew decided to take a walk. He strolled through the church garden and out to the main road.

Instead of taking a right and heading toward the French Quarter, he took a left, walked a half mile, turned right, and headed toward the Mississippi River. Reaching the great river, Father Andrew reflected on his sermon and the impact of his last statement, "Hillary Chollet is a fine example of a soldier of God." He remembered the reason he was here—a mission set forth by Saint Hilary of Poitiers. Carrying mixed feelings, as if he were being pulled in different directions—between the conscious and subconscious—he prayed to God to help him. Father Andrew was happy where he was and enjoyed being a coach and teaching young people mathematics. Weighing in as well were his friendships with Sister Madeline, the other sisters, and Father Solomon. Andrew decided to take a "wait and see" approach.

Returning home, Father Andrew was met by the sisters, who were all crying. They had found twelve-year-old Whitney dead in her little doggie bed. Andrew reminisced with the sisters and touchingly spoke about how in 1938, just after his arrival, he had found Whitney down by the fishing boats.

"Once I picked her up, she put her head on my chest and fell asleep and started to snore."

Everyone laughed and cried at the same time. Whitney was buried with full honors, and the sisters and Father Andrew gave her one last blessing.

CHAPTER 23

ᏜᎾ

F ather Andrew continued his coaching, teaching, and priestly
duties. One Sunday in March 1950, Hillary called and said he
was graduating from Cornell and had received an offer to play professional basketball. In addition, the Cleveland Rams had drafted
him for football, and he had received an offer to play professional
football in the Canadian Football League and to attend McGill
University for medical school. Hillary also said he had been accepted at Cornell medical school and that since the school was in
New York City, he thought that would offer him his best medical
training opportunity. He also told Father Andrew that he wanted
to be a surgeon.

Andrew told Hillary he was quite pleased with his news and
sometime in the near future he looked forward to meeting up with
him and reminiscing. A few months later, the monsignor at Cornell
called Father Andrew and told him that the following Saturday

afternoon on TV there would be a newsreel showing Hillary as an all-American selection.

Saturday afternoon came, and Father Solomon and the three sisters sat together in the great room around the TV. The program started. "Hello everybody, this is Bob Hall, your Touchdown Sports telecaster," the announcer said. "We're at Touchdown's all-American selection board meeting, where we'll announce the players to be named to this year's team. Around the table from left to right are George Corrigan, Louis Kelvin, C.D. Chesley, and yours truly. Before making our decisions, we studied action films of fifty-seven leading college football teams and viewed more than one hundred thousand feet of film. First we present Hillary Chollet of Cornell. He weighs one hundred and eighty-five pounds and stands six feet tall. He attended Holy Cross High School in New Orleans and just completed his fourth year as a mainstay of the Big Red backfield. He is an outstanding basketball player and is considered one of Cornell's greatest all-time athletes.

"Chollet does everything well, including throwing the leather. Coach Lefty James and his staff, as well as his teammates, regard Chollet as a players' player, always at his best when the going is at its roughest. Hillary Chollet is a fine example for the young people of our nation, for this all-American, in his spare time, is an orderly in a hospital for polio victims, and he is a hero in the eyes of all kids who come in contact with him either at his work or through the medium of sports.

"Now let's see him in game action in the Penn-Cornell Game. On the receiving end is Chollet. The brilliant Cornell back takes the pass and moves downfield and chalks up another fifty-yard gain for the Big Red. Now in the Yellow game, the Bulldogs kick off. On the six-yard line, Chollet gathers it in…and watch him move up field. Aided by good blocking, he breaks into the clear, and it looks as if he may go the distance. They finally knock him out of bounds after he's gone fifty-six yards. Chollet plays both offensive and defensive football, and his ability to diagnose plays and intercept forward passes makes him invaluable. Chollet takes it and…watch this terrific runback. Reversing his field, this great back wheels off another long gain for his teammates from far above Cayuga Waters.

"Now we'll see Chollet score one of his many touchdowns. Teammate Bernie Babula has the ball that he laterals to Chollet. Watch as this all-American turns it on and goes over to score."

After watching the newsreel, the five clergy members all felt proud. Over the coming days and weeks, Father Andrew knew his time was growing short at Holy Cross. He spoke with Father Solomon, who also knew there was a change coming in the near future. Sister Madeline felt a little nervous over the potential news that was unspoken but felt by everyone.

CHAPTER 24

꧁

A s the subsequent weeks and months passed, Sister Madeline felt an increasing restlessness. The anticipation was bearable, but how fast time went by made her situation almost unbearable. She reflected back several months when, after dinner, Father Andrew was going for a walk, and she asked him if she could join him. Father Andrew replied, "Well, of course, Sister."

While on their walk, Andrew told her about a letter he had written in his journal. He asked her if she would like to hear it, and she said, "Yes, Father."

Fresh in her mind, as if it were yesterday, Sister Madeline remembered the words, and Andrew's voice, as he read his letter, which was titled, "The Carpet." Hearing the letter and the beautiful words and the humble nature by which they were delivered made Sister Madeline want to be one of the threads of the carpet, as long as Father Andrew was one of the threads too.

Wanting to honor her feelings, that day Sister Madeline decided to ask Father Solomon if in two Sundays she could give the homily. This was unprecedented, but Father Solomon trusted Sister Madeline so much that he said, "Yes, Sister, you can."

Sister Madeline felt inspired, yet a little confused by her feelings over the whole matter of what she wanted to talk about in the homily. Sunday came, and Father Solomon started the Mass in the usual way. When it came time for the Bible passage and homily, he said, "We have a special speaker today. I'm honored to introduce my colleague and friend, Sister Madeline."

Stepping into the pulpit, Sister Madeline began, "Thank you, Father Solomon. I am honored for the opportunity to speak before this congregation. I will be reading from Corinthians, chapter thirteen, verses one through thirteen.

" 'If I speak in the tongues of men and of angels, but have not love, I am only a resounding gong or a clanging cymbal. If I have the gift of prophecy and can fathom all mysteries and all knowledge, and if I have a faith that can move mountains, but have not love, I am nothing. If I give all I possess to the poor and surrender my body to the flames, but have not love, I gain nothing. Love is patient, love is kind. It does not envy, it does not boast, it is not proud. It is not rude, it is not self-seeking, it is not easily angered, it keeps no record of wrongs. Love does not delight in evil but rejoices with the truth. It always protects, always trusts, always hopes, always perseveres. Love never fails. But where there are prophecies, they will cease; where there are tongues, they will be stilled; where there is knowledge, it will pass away. For we know in part and we prophesy in part, but when perfection comes, the imperfect disappears. When I was a child, I talked like a child, I thought like a child, I reasoned like a child. When I became a man, I put childish ways behind me. Now we see but a poor reflection as in a mirror; then we shall see face to face. Now I know in part; then I shall know fully, even as I am fully known. And now these three remain: faith, hope, and love. But the greatest of these is love.' "

Finishing the Bible passage, Sister Madeline waited a few seconds and then said, "Thanks be to God. Please be seated." Collecting her thoughts, she continued, "One Sunday Father Andrew spoke about Hillary Chollet and how he is a soldier of God. I don't disagree with that, but I want to give testament to the fact that there are other soldiers of God here. It may be, and probably is, that every one of us is a soldier of God. It's just that a period of self-discovery is needed for some of us to figure this out."

Sister Madeline said she would like to give honor to the women of Grandma Knows Best. Everyone in the audience clapped, because they all knew the good work Sister Madeline and the program had done.

Madeline said, "These grandmas are soldiers. In particular, when this program was started, there was a woman who, when she was just a little girl, learned she had a first name but didn't have a last name. Her name was Rosa. She was a slave. When she was ten years old, the brother of her owner befriended her and taught her to read. Years later, when Rosa was twenty, she fell in love with this man. He gave her his first name as her last name and gave her 'pretend parents.' Rosa and Michael had a child named Olivia.

As you know, Olivia and Rosa ran a farm just outside of town, and of course, they both have passed away, but the work they did for Grandma Knows Best by helping raise many children made them soldiers of God.

"Lastly I would like to honor Father Andrew, whom you all know and love. He too is a soldier of God."

The entire congregation felt the message from Corinthians and Sister Madeline. As they applauded, Sister Madeline blushed. She looked back at Father Andrew, who felt proud and very close to Madeline. The service ended, and the sisters and the priests met the congregation and shook their hands one by one.

After Mass they went back to the rectory. Father Solomon felt very proud of Sister Madeline, as did Sister Mary, Sister Margaret, and Father Andrew.

CHAPTER 25

✲

On May 1, 1955, Father Andrew woke up, as he usually did, around six in the morning, did his meditational prayer, had his typical breakfast of two oranges and one banana, and made his way to school. Basketball season had ended, and the kids were counting the days to the end of school. The freshmen, sophomores, and juniors worked hard because they were still in high school and had yet to be determined futures.

Across the city, however, senior students were in a daydream state. Some of the girls were aflutter because they didn't know what they were going to do after graduation and some because they were experiencing first love. Most of the boys were looking for jobs, but some were blessed with having been accepted into colleges both far and near.

After school that day, Father Andrew walked back to the great room in the rectory to check his mail. In a reflective mood, he stood under the arched entrance and looked into the empty room. He felt comforted by seeing the great fireplace, comfortable chairs, and big couch. Many a conversation had been shared there by Father Andrew and Father Solomon, as well as Father Andrew and the sisters and in particular Father Andrew and Sister Madeline. Father Andrew went to the side table behind the sofa and got his mail. One envelope caught his eye. It was addressed to Father Andrew. The return address was Montclair, New Jersey. The envelope itself was a unique sight, as it looked very formal and elegant, as if it might have come from the president or a head of state.

Father Andrew carefully opened the envelope and removed its contents. As he did he saw that it was an invitation to a wedding. Father Andrew's heart beat a little faster as he realized he'd been invited to the wedding of Hillary Chollet and Janet Dingwall. The wedding was to take place June 14, 1955, in Ithaca, New York, at the Chapel at Newman Oratory.

Father Andrew had been corresponding with Monsignor Cleary for several years. Most recently he knew Hillary had graduated from medical school in New York City and was a surgery intern at Bellevue Hospital. This was the first time Father Andrew had heard about Janet Dingwall, but he was sure that both Hillary and Janet were lucky to have each other. Besides the invitation, there was a little note written by Janet Dingwall.

The note read:

> *Dear Father Andrew,*
>
> *Hillary and I would be proud to have you at our wedding. Hardly a week goes by without Hillary mentioning you. We all*

feel an enormous gratitude for all you have done for him. Both Hillary and I would like you, Father Andrew, before we say our vows, to give us a blessing on the altar. Monsignor Cleary will be joining us in matrimony. Please give us a call at Montclair 76432 at your earliest convenience.

Respectfully,

Janet Dingwall

Father Andrew carefully folded the note and placed both note and invitation back into the envelope. Thinking about the news of the wedding, and daydreaming about his time in New Orleans, he returned his attention to the present, as he thought, *I'd better call Janet right now.* He took the note back out of the envelope, reread it, and then focused on the telephone number. He picked up the phone and dialed "0."

Ring, ring, ring...

"Hello. Operator."

"Hello, my name is Father Andrew, and I need to make a long-distance call."

"What's the number, Father?"

"Montclair 76432."

"Thank you, sir. Now dialing. Have a nice day."

After a few rings, a woman's voice came on the line. "Hello?"

"Hello, this is Father Andrew calling from New Orleans. Is Janet Dingwall home?"

"Hello, Father. I'm sorry. She isn't. This is her mother, Ariel. Janet is at work in New York City. I bet you're calling about the wedding. I'm helping with some of the arrangements."

Andrew thought how charming and thoughtful Ariel sounded, and he believed he detected a French Canadian accent. He added, "As a matter of fact, I am. Could you please relay to Janet and Hillary that I will be at the wedding and would be honored to give them a blessing during the ceremony just before their vows?"

Ariel said, "I'm so glad to hear that, Father. I'll tell Janet about our conversation, and Father, I would like to personally thank you for all that you've done for Hillary. He's such a fine young man."

Father Andrew said, "I couldn't agree more, Mrs. Dingwall. Thank you for the kind words."

After saying good-bye, Father Andrew went into the church to pray. As he finished he looked up at the cross and Jesus and re-membered some of Jesus's last spoken words. "*Tetelestai*" was one of his last spoken words in Hebrew, meaning, "It is finished." In Greek it translated to "I have come in my season full of glory." Andrew reflected on his seventeen years at Holy Cross and thought the Greek translation in a small way applied to him and that one way or another his time there was growing short.

At dinner that night, Father Andrew told the three sisters and Father Solomon that on June 9 he would be traveling to Ithaca, New York, by train. Everyone seemed very happy for Hillary and Janet, but the happiness of the situation was replaced by quiet, as an unspoken reality set in. It appeared to everyone that Father Andrew was destined perhaps not to return.

Sister Madeline, fighting back tears, broke the silence. "Well, that settles it," she said. "We'll have a going-away party for Father Andrew on the night of June eighth."

That night Father Andrew hardly slept a wink. He lay in bed and thought and thought about his time in New Orleans. He had arrived in August 1938, and now it was May 1, 1955. Nearly seventeen years had passed. In his mind he knew that he was on a mission, but the exact particulars of his past were hidden deep within his brain. This area felt like the wing of a library with rows and rows of untouchable books filled with memories, times, and places. In his heart, Father Andrew felt an increasing sense of wanting to go home, but he didn't know exactly where his home was.

CHAPTER 26

⊙⟩⟩⟩⟩⟩⟩⟩⟨⟨⊙

The next few weeks of school flew by, and before Father Andrew knew it, the eighth of June was upon Holy Cross Church. It was early evening, about six o'clock, and he had finished his meditative walk, spent a few minutes in the garden, and returned to the church to get ready for dinner. After washing his hands and face, he sat down for ten minutes and wrote in his journal and then returned it to his suitcase, which was the same one he had arrived with some seventeen years ago. Now he had six books filled with his impressions and thoughts. Taking a breath and exhaling with a big sigh, Father Andrew closed his suitcase and headed to the rectory.

As he entered the big room, he was met by Father Solomon. Ever the stickler for detail, he said, "Father Andrew, this coming Sunday I want to try something new. Can you give me ten minutes? I'd like to try it out on you."

Even though Father Andrew had a thousand things on his mind, instinctively he said, "Of course, Father."

The two walked through the rectory, through the kitchen, into the back room, and down a narrow corridor that emptied into the church near the pulpit. Father Andrew and Father Solomon walked to the pulpit, turned, and faced Jesus on the cross.

Father Solomon said in a whisper to Father Andrew, "Please turn around. This is your going-away party!"

As Father Andrew turned around, his eyes fell upon the entire congregation, and a party inside the church ensued. For about an hour, Father Solomon turned over the pulpit to the members of the congregation. Father Andrew and Father Solomon sat in the first row of pews as person after person gave testimony to their experiences with Father Andrew. Laughter and joking rang throughout the church, and it was apparent that everyone was proud of Father Andrew. Snacks, punch, and lemonade were served for all to enjoy.

Proud and humbled by the kind words and love that his congregation and his coworkers had sent his way, Father Andrew gave thanks to all. He retired for the night and fell deeply asleep.

CHAPTER 27

∽∾

The following morning, Father Andrew's train was scheduled to leave at ten. It would be a long trip, first from New Orleans to Chicago, then Chicago to Buffalo, and finally from Buffalo to Ithaca, New York. It would take nearly two-and-a-half days to make the journey.

By eight that morning, Father Andrew had finished packing his suitcase. Dressed in his black suit, clerical collar, and Sunday shoes, he carried his suitcase to the great room in the rectory. As he sat on the couch in front of the fireplace, for the first time he felt like a visitor going home. He was happy he was going to Hillary and Janet's wedding, but at the same time felt a wave of emotion, including a sick feeling in the pit of his stomach.

Father Solomon, Sister Madeline, Sister Mary, and Sister Margaret were all going to take Father Andrew to the train station.

Father Solomon had traded in his Model T Ford and bought a 1954 Pontiac, a real beauty.

Father Solomon said, "Andrew, I'll pull the car around and meet you out front."

Solomon went outside to get the car while the sisters headed to the foyer. Each one stopped and gave Father Andrew a good-bye hug and a kiss on the cheek, and then headed out to the awaiting car. After Sister Margaret and Sister Mary went outside, that left just Father Andrew and Sister Madeline. With a tear in her eye, she walked up to Father Andrew, looked him in the eyes, and hugged him. As Father Andrew went to kiss her on the cheek, somehow their lips brushed. For an instant, plus one or two seconds, they froze, lips touching lips, heart touching heart, each able to feel the other's thumping heartbeat. It was a feeling Father Andrew hadn't experienced during his time in New Orleans. Head spinning, he was reminded of a similar experience he'd had, but he couldn't remember the time, date, or situation. Trying to remember, he could tell that the memory in question was in a closed wing of his mind's library of memories. It was a faraway, pleasant memory with feeling and sound—like the sound of a faraway train whistle softly heard in the cool of night. After the kiss and touching of lips, their eyes could not lie. Sister Madeline and Father Andrew had strong feelings for each other.

Sister Madeline wondered, *Was this kiss wrong? Was it a bite from the apple?* She started to get nervous, and Father Andrew saw this and said, "Madeline, it's OK." He put his arm around Sister Madeline and tried to comfort her. Arm in arm, as they walked the last five steps to the door, both wished the five-step journey would take a lifetime.

CHAPTER 28

᷈᷈᷈

They all loaded into the Pontiac and drove to the train station. Ticket and suitcase in hand, wedding invitation tucked into his inside coat pocket, Father Andrew said his final good-byes and headed to the boarding area. Sister Margaret gave him two oranges and one banana as a gift for the train ride.

"All aboard!" the conductor called out.

Father Andrew marveled at the size and power of the train before him. Somewhat of a train buff, he recognized the train known as the *City of New Orleans*. It was part of the Illinois Central Railroad. Streamlined, and sporting the Illinois Central livery in chocolate brown and orange with yellow trim, the train was a two-thousand-horsepower diesel locomotive. On the platform, Father Andrew stepped up to the conductor and handed him his ticket.

"Head down to the next car," the conductor told him. "That's the entrance for whites."

As Father Andrew walked toward the entrance for whites, an unsettled feeling poured through his system. He remembered reading in the newspaper that just recently, on May 31, the US Supreme Court had ordered that states "must end racial segregation with all deliberate speed." Away from the comfort of Holy Cross, he knew there was still bias and prejudice among people.

Boarding the train via the white entrance, Father Andrew climbed up the three steps that led him into his car. Once on the train, he turned left and entered a hallway area. In his car it looked like there were about thirty rows, with a center aisle and two seats on each side of the aisle. In the first twenty rows, he saw nicely dressed women and men. Some of the men were smoking cigars; a few had families with little kids. There seemed to be open seats, but as Father Andrew would try to take an open seat, each person would say, "Sorry...saved."

Father Andrew made it to the last ten rows in the car, where there appeared to be an unmarked but understood line between the whites and the blacks. He saw one open seat and took it. It was next to a lady by the window in the black section. She appeared to be in her twenties and had beautiful Creole-colored skin. He couldn't help notice that this woman was very pregnant.

Squeezing into his seat, Andrew placed his suitcase under the seat in front of him and held Sister Margaret's fruit in his lap. Once settled he turned to the lady next to him, extended his hand, and introduced himself.

"Hello, my name is Father Andrew."

A little nervous, the lady shook his hand. "Hello, sir. My name is Jasmine."

It was 10:05 a.m. Father Andrew heard the final call, "All aboard!"

As the last passengers boarded, he heard the train whistle—several long, loud toots—which was the signal that this locomotive with seventeen cars and one caboose was on its way to Chicago.

Father Andrew couldn't remember the last time he had been on a train without any responsibility. As he coached the boys through the years, they occasionally got to go by train when they played in Baton Rouge, which was about seventy miles from New Orleans.

Once the train was underway, Father Andrew slipped out of his Sunday shoes and placed his feet on top of his suitcase. He wiggled his toes and looked at their movements. Not wanting to draw attention, Andrew checked his surroundings and travel companions, looking to the left and ahead of him, then turning his head toward the back of the car.

Seeing the stark line of separation between whites and blacks, Andrew knew he had trouble treating people differently based on the color of their skin. As he thought back to the time of Jesus's birth, he realized even the Three Wise Men from the East had dark skin. In sports the racial lines were disappearing. In 1947 Jackie Robinson had broken the color barrier by playing for the Brooklyn Dodgers.

Father Andrew thought that Ezra Day, the president of Cornell, along with his wife, had made a progressive, insightful decision to accept Hillary after Tulane had turned him down for having skin they considered to be too dark.

He heard lots of laughing and joking coming from several rows in front of him; even though the train had just started, the service waiter already was handing out drinks. The waiter reached the last row of white people and could see that Father Andrew wasn't sitting in the white section. He didn't quite know what to do because he wasn't supposed to offer drinks to the people behind the line of whites. Crossing the line he asked, "Father, would you like something to drink?" Father Andrew politely answered, "No, thank you."

Jasmine struck up a conversation with Father Andrew. She felt out of sorts, being eight-and-a-half months pregnant; she felt like she was ready to explode. "Father," she said, "which church do you work at?"

Andrew replied, "I work at Holy Cross. For the past seventeen years, I've coached the football and basketball teams, along with teaching mathematics."

"That's interesting, Father. My husband is a sportswriter in Chicago. I work as an elementary school teacher. Last week my aunt, Bessie, passed away, so I came to New Orleans to attend the funeral. My husband, Thomas, didn't want me to travel, since I'm so close to having the baby."

Father Andrew said, "I'm going to a wedding in Ithaca, New York. My trip goes to Chicago, then Buffalo, then finally, Ithaca."

The train lumbered along, first through Louisiana, then through parts of Kentucky and Tennessee. Although the train was moving at only about fifty miles an hour, the bantering of the people in front made it difficult for Father Andrew to snooze. As the hours passed, the people in front became louder as they drank more. The trip from New Orleans to Chicago would take about eighteen hours. With several stops along the way, the arrival time in Chicago was five in the morning. Father Andrew looked at his watch and could see it was 5:00 p.m.

The porter handed out box dinners to everyone in front of them but didn't hand out any to the people in his group. Jasmine had a little bag with a Louisiana spicy sausage and some cheese and crackers. She asked Father Andrew if he would like some. He brought out his bag of two oranges and one banana, and the two decided to have a picnic on the train. They enjoyed their appetizer of oranges, then their entrée of cheese, crackers, and hot sausage. For dessert they split the banana.

After their feast the drone of the train engines and the *click, click, click* of the wheels on the track lulled them both to sleep. Father Andrew fell into a deep sleep, but around 10:00 p.m. he was awakened by two sensations. First was the sound of moaning from Jasmine; the other was a wet feeling underneath his behind, which seemed to be coming from Jasmine's side of the seat. He opened his eyes and saw concern on her face. Having already had one child, she knew what had just happened and also knew what was going to happen.

At first Father Andrew was in a state of panic, but then he remembered his "quiet eyes"; he quickly squeezed the webbed space between his index finger and his thumb—first the left hand then the right. A calm mind would allow his know-how to come to the surface. Just as he had years ago, when he had helped Billy after the men in zoot suits had stabbed him, Father Andrew thought, *This isn't a good situation.*

Jasmine said, "Father, my water broke."

Father Andrew knew he would have to take the lead. Eyeing the porter, he flagged him down and said, "Sir, this woman next to me—my friend—is going to have a baby."

The porter said, "Well, that's nice to hear."

Father Andrew said, "No, you don't understand. She's going to have a baby—on this train—*now*. How far away are we from Chicago?"

The porter said, "We won't be in Chicago for another seven hours. There's one town that's about three-and-a-half hours away, but until then there are no stopping points."

Jasmine let out a big groan—the type of groan any doctor or nurse or any woman who has had a baby would recognize, a groan from a contraction that was just short of a bloodcurdling scream. It woke up the entire car.

Father Andrew stood up and said, "Everyone, my name is Father Andrew, and my friend here, Jasmine, is going into labor. She's going to have a baby within the next ten or fifteen minutes."

Everyone in the car was in shock. At the very front of the car, in the white section, a couple had started arguing. Nicely dressed, the woman obviously came from a wealthy background. The man was dressed in an expensive-looking suit and appeared to be one of the fellows who had been drinking. The upset woman finally said, "I don't care what you say." She then marched right down the aisle to Father Andrew and said, "Father, I'm a nurse. How can I help?"

Father Andrew said, "Thanks for your help. What's your name?"

The young nurse, already holding Jasmine's hand and feeling her pulse, said, "I'm Barbara."

Thinking of his next step, Andrew said, "Let's move her up front where she can lie down."

Up front there was a fold-down couch that the porters used on overnight trips when there was low passenger volume. It was the perfect fold-down for the delivery. Two of the men in Father Andrew's section helped lift Jasmine and bring her to the couch.

The porter came and brought some clean linens from the Pullman sleeper car, and Father Andrew took out his pocket watch just as he heard Jasmine say, "Another one is coming, Father!"

Father Andrew glanced at his watch; only ninety seconds had passed since the first contraction. He knew that with second, third, and fourth pregnancies, the baby could come a lot sooner. He talked it over with the nurse, and they decided they'd better take a look at what was going on.

With clean towels and hot water, they washed their hands and positioned Jasmine so they could get a good look. Father Andrew didn't have sterile gloves, but he knew he had to do an exam, so with Nurse Barbara standing by, they checked her and felt that the cervix was at nine centimeters and was completely effaced, which meant the birth canal was 100 percent open.

"This baby is coming soon," Father Andrew said.

As the nurse coached Jasmine in her breathing, she revealed a little bit about herself. She was a new graduate nurse who worked at Cook County Hospital in Chicago. She had OB experience from her training just six months ago and worked in the emergency room. Cook County was one of those institutions where doctors and nurses learned by "See one, do one, teach one." Barbara continued to work with Jasmine on her breathing as the contractions came.

After another two contractions, Jasmine said, "Oh my God, the baby is coming!"

Father Andrew knew this delivery was going to take place whether he liked it or not. Remembering that newborns were very slippery, he thought, *Once this baby comes, I don't want to drop it.*

By now everyone in the white section was watching along with everyone in the black section, and for once they all seemed to be on the same side. There was a sense of unity for the human condition and the birth of this child.

Jasmine screamed, "Oh, Father, here comes another contraction!"

Father Andrew said, "Oh, Lord, here it comes. Push, Jasmine, push." After the baby started to come out, he supported the head. The child had a lot of hair but was on the small side. Once the head was completely out, Father could see that the cord was wrapped around its neck.

He inserted two of his fingers between the baby and the cord and pushed on the baby's head a little with his palm and prevented the baby from coming out any farther. By doing so he was able to slide the cord over the baby's head, which allowed the left shoulder to come out, then the right shoulder; then the rest of the baby popped out.

Father Andrew said, "Jasmine, it's a girl." He said to the porter, "Give me a straw."

He told Barbara to put the straw into the baby's mouth and suck. She did so, and almost immediately the baby started to cough. Then he said, "Put the straw into each nostril and suck."

Barbara did so, and the baby started to cry. The one minute Apgar score was 10! Her **a**ppearance, **p**ulse, **g**rimace, **a**ctivity, and **r**espirations were all good. Father Andrew held the little girl and placed her on top of Jasmine's belly; the baby was still connected by its umbilical cord. Barbara's husband was now peering, as was everyone else.

Father Andrew said to him, "Sir, give me your shoelace."

The man didn't bat an eye. He took off his shoe, unthreaded his shoelace, and handed it to Father Andrew, who dipped it into the man's glass of Scotch and then tied off the umbilical cord close to the baby's belly button. He put another tie on the mother's side and cut the cord with his pocketknife. He handed the baby to Barbara, and she bundled up the little girl in a small blanket. The newborn, which was at first very slippery, was wiped dry and fortunately had what Father Andrew remembered as a very good five minute Apgar score for complexion, pulse rate, reflex/irritability, muscle tone, and breathing.

Barbara placed the bundled-up baby on Jasmine's chest. Father Andrew knew he had to massage the uterus and deliver the placenta, remembering that if this placenta did not come out, the woman could bleed to death. It seemed like an eternity, but eventually, after he massaged the uterus, the entire placenta came out. Everyone cheered, and at least for an instant, the lines of race and color disappeared and all were united.

After the baby was born, Jasmine felt pretty good. She started to breastfeed her little girl and felt she could actually make it all the way to Chicago.

When the train arrived in Chicago, Father Andrew and Barbara, along with her shoelace-less husband, helped the mother and child off the train and into the waiting arms of her husband, Thomas, the sportswriter.

She said to her husband, "This man, Father Andrew, and Nurse Barbara helped me. They saved me and our baby girl."

Thomas shook their hands and was very thankful. Father Andrew made sure the mother and baby girl were both safe. Then he blessed them and headed back to the train, which was departing for Buffalo. Once in Buffalo, he got on another train headed to Ithaca. As soon as the train left the station, he fell asleep.

Some five hours later, Father Andrew felt a gentle touch on his shoulder. "Father, we're here," the porter said. "We're in Ithaca."

CHAPTER 29

ᏟᎥᏖᎥᏐ

Father Andrew took a deep breath as he stepped off the train with his brown suitcase in his left hand. Hillary and Janet were waiting for him. They walked toward Father Andrew and threw their arms around him. Hillary shook his hand, and Father Andrew exclaimed, "Hillary and Janet, I sure am glad to see you! Janet, I'm so glad to meet you. Congratulations on being engaged and on your wedding tomorrow!"

Hillary took Father Andrew's suitcase. Janet grabbed him by the arm and slid her arm around his, and they walked toward the main station. Father Andrew could see Hillary had developed into a man. From that kid with no shoes until now—well, it was quite the transformation. Despite Hillary's six-foot-tall, 185-pound frame, Andrew was reminded of the shy nature he had first seen when they had met back in 1938. Back then Hillary was twelve years old, and he was thirty-two years old. Now, seventeen years later, Father Andrew reflected on his own age of forty-nine and the fact that he was ever so slightly starting to feel his age. Hillary and Janet were both twenty-nine years old and looked like they had the whole world before them. Father Andrew looked at Janet, who was dressed in a knee-length yellow sundress and flat shoes. She had neatly cropped long brown hair, blue eyes, and the silkiest skin he had ever seen. Andrew felt those were eyes that could melt a person and probably any situation. Janet had a beautiful smile, with lips outlined by pink lipstick; her nails were painted with red polish. She spoke in a quiet voice with the slightest hint of a New England accent.

Hillary said, "Father, our wedding is at the Newman Center in the little chapel tomorrow at two. Monsignor Cleary will be marrying us. He's made arrangements for you to stay in the quarters reserved for visiting guests and clergy. I know you must be tired after your long trip, but we'd like to take you out to lunch."

Father Andrew said, "I'm famished."

As they piled into the car that Hillary had borrowed from his best man, Anthony Gasioni, they began the three-minute trip to a little café just off the Cornell campus. Le Petit Café stood on a street corner; the warm late-spring sun helped the trio choose an outside table with an umbrella. There was a little bit of a breeze, and it was definitely a warm day. After they sat down, the waitress took their orders. Janet asked for an iced tea and a grilled cheese sandwich, Hillary asked for a Coca-Cola and a burger, and Father Andrew said, "That sounds good. I'll have the same, but make mine a cheeseburger. Oh, and I'll have water."

After they ordered, Father Andrew began the conversation by asking, "How did you two meet?"

Janet said, "Well, Father, we met right here at Cornell. We were attending Cornell at the same time and were both seniors. One day at the Student Union Bookstore, while looking for books, we met for the first time. At the time I didn't even know Hillary was a football and basketball star. I took a liking to his shy, quiet approach; his ease with conversation; and his soulful background. First we became friends. Then we started dating, and our romance evolved. Over the last four years, Father, I won't say that there haven't been some rough spots, but overall it's been wonderful. While Hillary was in medical school in New York City, I took a job as the assistant fashion editor of the Cotton Council of America also in New York City. Last year my mom and dad sent me on a vacation to Europe, and when I got back, Hillary proposed to me."

Hillary picked up where Janet left off. "Father, training in medicine is a real undertaking and, as you know, I like to complete something once I start. Because my mom and dad's marriage didn't work out so well, I wanted to make sure things worked out for me and my wife-to-be. Father, I'm blessed to have found such a wonderful woman as Janet." Hillary then said, "Father, in case you're wondering why we're getting married here at Cornell instead of New York City, well, Janet is Protestant and, as you know, I'm Catholic. None of the Catholic churches in New York City would marry us, but Monsignor Cleary felt that because we loved each other, and since we're both Christians, it would be OK for us to have a Catholic wedding in the chapel at the Newman Center.

Monsignor Cleary has a special sense, one that's more inclusive than the traditional rules of the Catholic Church."

Father Andrew could tell, after this conversation, that although it didn't really matter to him, it was apparent that Hillary came from the other side of the railroad tracks, while Janet had a wealthier background. He laughed to himself, thinking, *I too come from the other side.*

After lunch the couple took the priest to the Cornell campus. Father Andrew was amazed at the sight of this Ivy League school. As they drove past the football stadium, he said, "Hillary, back at Holy Cross, we saw many of your games on television."

Returning the kudos, Hillary said, "Well, Father, you were my first coach, and you're still my mentor."

Janet added, "Father, if we ever have a son, 'Andrew' will be his middle name."

Upon reaching the Newman Center, they took Father Andrew to Monsignor Cleary's office. Hillary and Janet introduced the two men, and the couple said good-bye. Father Andrew thanked Hillary and Janet for meeting him at the train station and told them he was looking forward to the wedding tomorrow.

Monsignor Cleary shook Father Andrew's hand and said, "Welcome, Andrew. Please call me Donald. Welcome to Ithaca, and welcome to the Newman Oratory. I'll show you your room, which is very close to the church."

The monsignor gave Andrew a tour of the Newman Oratory. He showed him the chapel and said, "We'll meet tomorrow at one o'clock to go over things before the wedding." As Monsignor

Cleary showed Father Andrew to his room, he said, "Oh, and tomorrow Bishop Michael will be at the ceremony. He's visiting from New York City, and although, in the hierarchy of our church, he's way up there, he doesn't have the all-inclusive nature we have here at Cornell and at the Newman Oratory."

Upon reaching his room, the monsignor opened the door and said, "Andrew, this is your room. You don't need a key, and you're free to come and go. I'll meet you in the church at one o'clock tomorrow. It's a tradition here at the Newman Oratory for visitors to place their shoes outside the door at night; by the next morning your shoes will be polished."

His words made Father Andrew feel at home, because that was the same statement Father Solomon had made to him seventeen years ago.

Andrew shook Monsignor Cleary's hand and went into his room and unpacked his suitcase. After he hung up his clothes, he took out his six journals. At the bottom of the suitcase, for the first time in a long time, he picked up the little round box, removed the top, and turned it upside down; out fell the gold coin. The weight of the coin caused his outstretched hand to fall downward a few inches. He eyed the coin. On one side he saw a picture of the cosmos. As he flipped the coin, he was reminded of his meeting with Saint Hilary. On the reverse side of the coin, he saw the image of Jesus as God. He remembered that when he was with Saint Hilary he had an all-inclusive feeling when viewing the coin and thought that to another the image of God might take on a different form.

Reflecting deeply, Father Andrew told himself that it was time for him to deliver this coin, as requested by Saint Hilary. He admitted to himself that for several years now he knew that Hillary was the person to which Saint Hilary had originally referred. Now, more than seventeen years later, it was time. At the wedding tomorrow after the blessing, he would give this special gift to Hillary.

Experiencing many emotions, he figured a long walk would help him think things through. Father Andrew saw the football stadium as he exited the Newman Oratory; he wanted to see the field where Hillary had played many a game. From his vantage point on top of a hill, he saw the entire stadium and empty field. There was no one in sight, and it was quiet except for the slight whistle from a developing wind. As he listened to the wind and looked at the field, the sound of the wind started to sound like cheering fans. The empty field came alive, and Andrew saw the fresh chalk lines that outlined the field. He imagined seeing the stadium full. A play started, and the opposing team threw a long pass, which was intercepted by a player wearing number twenty-two on his jersey. The announcer said, "Oh my! An interception by Chollet. He reverses his field, picks up a block, and look at him go. What a run—he may go all the way. He's finally pushed out of bounds... what a play! Add another fifty-seven yards to the Big Red defense and this all-American."

Suddenly Father Andrew heard a meow and felt something touch his leg. He looked down and saw an orange-and-white calico cat rubbing against his pants and gazing up at him. Andrew picked up the cat and rubbed her ears. Within ten seconds the kitty was purring. He noticed the cat was heavy and figured she was probably well fed by the supply of field mice around the stadium. Andrew put the cat down and said, "Off you go. God bless." Then he looked at his watch. Seeing that it was ten after six, he wondered where the time had gone and headed back to the Newman Center.

Cornell was huge, with many buildings across a sprawled campus and landscape. A few hundred yards from the field, Andrew saw a small eatery that was, of all things, an Irish pub. Hungry, he decided to grab a bite to eat. He entered the Luck of the Irish Pub and concluded that the football field was empty because everyone was in the pub. Inside, the lighting was dark, and for a moment Father Andrew could hardly see, but as his eyes adjusted, into focus came a sight straight from Dublin—a through-and-through Irish pub.

A hostess wearing a name tag that read, "Holly," said, "Good evening, Father. Would you like a table for dinner, or do you want to sit at the bar?

Father Andrew half-wondered what he was getting into, but he was hungry, so he said, "A table will be fine."

A jukebox was playing Rosemary Clooney's "This Ole House." As he walked past the bar to his table, a drunk fellow sitting at the bar saw him and asked, "Am I at church? Bless me, Father, for I have sinned. My last confession was in nineteen-zippity-doo."

The man busted out laughing, and the hostess admonished him, "Shut up, Michael, or I'll call your wife."

Father Andrew sat at a table in a quiet corner of the restaurant, where he was still able to hear the music. Tony Bennett was singing one of his favorites, "Stranger in Paradise." Still feeling a bit nervous about the events on the train, when asked what he'd like to drink, Father Andrew replied, "I'll have a glass of water and a large beer." He thought that the pub sort of reminded him of the French Quarter, and in a strange way, it gave him a feeling of being at home.

Enjoying the music, Andrew sipped his beer and water. He ordered the traditional corned beef and cabbage. Halfway through the meal, the server came over and said, "The tipsy man at the bar sends his apologies and wants you to have one of his favorite drinks." The server placed a large green beer and a shot of bourbon on the table. "It's a boilermaker, Father."

Slightly taken aback, Andrew thanked the server and finished his beer, then slowly finished his meal. Once done, he sat back, closed his eyes, and recounted the past week. A bit confused about his own past, present, and future, Father Andrew remembered having dinner with a Navy captain after the war. At dinner the officer had ordered a boilermaker and said, "Father, there's only one way to drink this. Drop the shot into the beer and drink it. It's called a depth charge." Father Andrew dropped the shot into the beer and downed it.

He looked at his watch and noted the time—7:20 p.m. At 7:26 he called the server and said, "I'm ready for my check." While waiting for the check, he wondered if it had been smart to drink the boilermaker the depth-charge way.

Enjoying the cool night air, he made his way back to his room and placed his Sunday shoes outside his door. He undressed, splashed some water on his face, and climbed into bed. Tired, he said a simple prayer and asked God to keep him safe and to bless Hillary and Janet at their wedding tomorrow.

CHAPTER 30

⊙⟊⟊⟊⊙

The next day the chirping of birds outside Andrew's window woke him. He saw that the sun was already high and checked his watch. A flash of panic coursed through his body as he saw that it was twelve thirty in the afternoon. Still half asleep, multiple questions went through his mind. *Did I miss the wedding?* He thought. *Am I in the right time zone?*

Collecting his thoughts, he realized he had twenty-nine minutes to get dressed and make it to the church, which fortunately was nearby. He quickly showered and shaved and then put on his suit, clerical collar, and socks. *Where are my shoes?* He wondered. *Oh yes!* He opened the door to his room and saw that his shoes were gone! He then thought *Holy smoke! I can't go to a wedding without shoes.* With no time to begin a long search for his shoes, Father Andrew looked in his suitcase and then remembered he had brought only one pair. Double-checking his memory, he looked in the closet—no shoes. Feeling a bit panicked, he exited his room, walked past two other guest rooms, and then headed into a part of the building that seemed to be a storage area. Andrew quickly scanned the room and saw a sink, a mop, and a row of lockers. Eight gym lockers, each about six feet tall, stood side by side.

He opened the first locker and saw some old uniforms; inside the second locker he found a bucket, a broom, and a mop; the third locker contained some gardening tools, an old jumpsuit, and at the bottom, an old muddy pair of shoes.

Andrew said, "Jackpot!" He picked up the shoes and thought, *This is my lucky day.* With only ten minutes to spare, he made the sign of the cross, looked up, and said, "Lord, forgive me. I have to borrow these shoes."

Andrew slid into the shoes, scraped off some of the mud, and was surprised they were a perfect fit. He raced back to his room, picked up the little round box with the gold coin, and placed it in his inside coat pocket.

He took the wedding invitation from his coat pocket and placed it in his back pants pocket. Barely having time to comb his hair and look in the mirror to make sure he was as presentable as possible, Father Andrew took one quick glance and noted his mostly gray hair. As he looked out the window, he saw a bush with several roses and two hummingbirds dancing around them. It briefly reminded him of the garden back at Holy Cross and gave him a good feeling. He glanced at his watch; it was 12:57 p.m., so he headed straight to the church. Monsignor Cleary was waiting for him.

"Ah! Father Andrew, good to see you."

The two fathers were talking when a third voice was heard. Monsignor Cleary turned to his right and said, "Bishop, glad to see you today."

Bishop Michael said, "I will be observing this wedding and will be off to the side. Perhaps, Monsignor Cleary, we can have a few words after the ceremony."

A little nervous, Monsignor Cleary raised his eyebrows a bit after the bishop left. He explained, "Now, Father, after the Mass, the ceremony will begin. Just before the vows, I'll give you a heads-up sign and say, 'And now Father Andrew will say a few words.' Any questions?" Father Andrew shook his head no. "Good. It's now one twenty. Meet me at this exact spot in thirty minutes."

Father Andrew said, "Thank you, Monsignor, for bringing me up to speed. I appreciate your hard work and the dedication you have as a fellow educator, working with students. I know how rewarding teaching is, and I also know how stressful it can be at times."

With thirty minutes until the wedding, Father Andrew left the church proper and decided to take a walk. Drawn to the little garden by the window in his room, he spotted a bench in the shade and sat down for a few minutes to collect his thoughts. After three or four minutes, he heard some footsteps, and looking to his left, he saw the bishop standing in front of him. The bishop cleared his throat.

Father Andrew stood up and bowed his head to the bishop, who asked, "Father, where are you from?"

"Holy Cross, in New Orleans."

The bishop said, "The Catholic Church is undergoing a lot of changes, some good and some not. Father, I'm sure you understand the importance of maintaining the doctrine of the Catholic Church."

Father Andrew nodded and said—perhaps in a way that Socrates would—"Hmmm. Yes, I see your point."

The bishop then said, "I don't approve of a marriage between a Catholic and a non-Catholic. After this ceremony, Monsignor Cleary and I will have a little talk. Changes will have to be made." The bishop then looked at Father Andrew from top to bottom. He stared directly at *those* shoes Father Andrew was wearing. As the bishop moved his head from side to side, Father Andrew got the feeling that his side-to-side nod was not bewilderment; rather it was disapproval. Bishop Michael then promptly turned around and left.

Father Andrew felt that time was drawing close to the wedding. He decided to go back inside through a different entrance so he wouldn't run into the bishop again. On the other side of the church, there was a door that led back inside. Already ajar, the door swung open with a noticeable creaking sound. Father Andrew went inside and walked down a hallway with rooms on either side. As he reached the end of the hallway, a light came on above one of the doors; it had a little sign that read, SAINT HILARY OF POITIERS.

Father Andrew opened the door and entered. There, sitting in a chair, was the very same Saint Hilary of Poitiers he had met seventeen years earlier. Saint Hilary invited him in. "Please sit down, Father Andrew."

Andrew felt a bit mystified as he looked at this saint who was born in three hundred A.D.

"Father Andrew, your time is growing short. Your mission is nearly complete. I know what you're planning to do, and this will complete your mission. You've done a fine job, and I know you are here to bless the wedding of Hillary and Janet. The good work of Monsignor Cleary will continue."

Saint Hilary of Poitiers took the pallium that hung around his neck and carefully wrapped it around Father Andrew's. This highly decorated scarf was made of lamb's wool and had gold lace trim; it was at least four feet long from end to end. Again speaking in French, Saint Hilary informed Andrew, "During your blessing, place this pallium first on Janet, then on Hillary, then back on yourself."

Father Andrew thanked Saint Hilary, although he didn't really know what would happen next. Saint Hilary extended his right hand to Father Andrew, and as Andrew reached for him, the saint placed his left hand on top of Andrew's hand. He spoke in a primordial language, one that Andrew did not understand, but he felt a magical blessing and believed that the saint was actually talking to God.

Practically walking on air, Father Andrew exited the room and looked at his watch—five minutes before two. He walked back into the church, and this time the little chapel was full of visitors, an organ player, a best man, and the matron of honor, Janet's mother,

Ariel. Father Andrew took his place and almost immediately both Bishop Michael and Monsignor Cleary came up to him.

The bishop took in his hand the scarf Andrew was wearing. As a religious historian, he knew this would be vestment dated back to the third century and was a relic for which the Vatican had been searching for more than 1,500 years. The bishop looked at Andrew again from head to toe and noticed the old shoes he was wearing. This time, however, the bishop felt humbled as he realized that those shoes, worn by Andrew, were just like the ones worn by a certain shepherd, and a certain carpenter. The vision of Jesus in those shoes overwhelmed the bishop, as he now believed the hand of God was at work here.

Monsignor Cleary had tears in his eyes. He knew that it wasn't Father Andrew particularly who was special but that the blessing and circumstance of the moment were ones of divine intervention.

The "Wedding March" began, and the beautiful bride entered. In no time Father Andrew heard Monsignor Cleary say, "And now Father Andrew will give a blessing."

The groom and bride were holding hands. Father Andrew took a moment to reflect on the beauty of the two and of this union that was about to take place.

It was then that Father Andrew remembered his past. All of the memories that had been hidden in "the dark library wing" suddenly became current memories—his entire past, including his career as a surgeon and the sad death of his mother. Fully aware that he was receiving a second chance to be with his mother, he felt blessed to actually be looking at her. The joy nearly overwhelmed him. With a tear in his eye and one running down his cheek, Father Andrew gave blessing to this matrimony, this union between a man and a woman. He blessed Janet and placed the scarf from Saint Hilary around her neck and gave her a blessing for life. Next he took the scarf and placed it around Hillary's neck and gave him a blessing for life.

While the scarf was still around Hillary, Father Andrew took from his pocket the little box with the coin and said, "Hillary and Janet, you are soldiers of God, and this symbol I give to you." He handed Hillary the box. "Son, please place this in your pocket."

Next Father Andrew took the scarf and placed it around his own neck and looked into the eyes of Janet, who was looking back into his eyes. He reached out with both hands. Hillary and Janet each took one of Father Andrew's hands. Janet squeezed his hand. Father Andrew savored the touch, because when his mother had died he was not even able to say good-bye. Feeling a sense of renewal and completeness, Father Andrew turned the ceremony back over to Monsignor Cleary. The bishop seemed glassy eyed, almost ready to pass out, as the circumstances at hand had transcended his level of thinking and coping.

Father Andrew went back to his seat, and as the ceremony finished, he heard, "You may now kiss the bride."

Next he heard wedding music as the couple exited the church. First the music was loud. Father Andrew looked toward the entrance of the church, where the sun was shining in, and as the music played, it grew quieter and quieter, and the sunlight pouring in through the front of the church grew brighter and brighter. Soon the music stopped, and everything around Father Andrew slowed down…down…down…

Still aware, he felt a breeze cross his face from right to left. This was followed by the bright sunlight turning into a white light. Father Andrew was then completely swept up by the white light.

CHAPTER 31

അന്ധ്യ

Several seconds later, Hillary realized he was back to his old self, and all of his memories had returned. In his mind's library all the lights were on. An extreme awareness developed; he had a clear recollection of what his mission had been and easily remembered the time he'd spent in the Ninth Ward of New Orleans, as well as his dear friends Father Solomon, Sister Margaret, Sister Mary, and Sister Madeline.

Thinking about Hillary and Janet's wedding; he knew Janet was his mother. Although he hadn't been able to say good-bye to her before she had died, as Father Andrew he was able to silently say that good-bye.

Hillary remembered his time spent in New Orleans as Father Andrew and also his two meetings with Saint Hilary. No longer wearing a suit and clerical collar, he was back in his scrubs and bloody booties.

Aware that he was back to being Hillary, his mind felt different. It felt better. His memory banks had an extra seventeen years' worth of memories and experiences. *How lucky*, he thought. The white light took him through the roof of the chapel and into a white-light tunnel. As each second passed, he felt his speed increase. Not able to see outside the tunnel, the doctor wondered, *What's next?*

The reality of this time-travel situation hit him, and he wondered if he had stayed in New Orleans and Hillary and Janet had a son, if he had been asked to do the baptism, would the baby he held have been himself? For a minute he imagined so and thought what he might have said to himself. All he could think of was "Have trust in yourself and ask God for help when needed."

Hillary continued his transport and readied himself for what he guessed was his next step. He recalled the trauma room in Los Angeles and the case of the young woman who had been shot in the chest and how he and Henry had repaired the two holes in her heart. Hillary groaned as he again felt the burns in his right hand and left foot that had occurred after the second defibrillation. That was when the woman's heart had started and his had stopped.

After another half minute or so, his speed of travel in the white light slowed down, and in the blink of an eye, he found himself once again out of body in the trauma room.

But this time his body wasn't in the same position as before. They had dragged him onto a gurney a few feet away from his dad. Sitting in his wheelchair, eyes wide open, his father watched helplessly as the doctors and nurses worked on his son, who was in cardiac arrest. The out-of-body Hillary looked around the whole room. His eyes focused on the clock, which read nineteen minutes after one. He remembered walking into the trauma room at around twelve twenty-five, but couldn't remember when the defibrillation had taken place. He thought, *It couldn't have been more than ten or fifteen minutes ago.* But how could he have experienced seventeen years in just ten or fifteen minutes?

Had he imagined it all? Is this what happened when the heart stopped and the brain became deprived of oxygen? Perhaps it was a mechanism, just like the Fourth of July and the explosion of fireworks. When the brain becomes extremely deprived of oxygen, as a last burst of energy to give nutrients and supply oxygen, it shoots off a cascade of everything it has—hormones and endorphins and would-be psychotropic substances leading to an entirely imagined event and white light.

Could this *all* be *not* real?

For a minute Hillary felt scared, but then his fear was replaced by sorrow when he once again looked down into the eyes of his dad as he stared at his son's limp, helpless body. Maureen's eyes were filled with terror as she clutched the elder Hillary's hand. She grasped his hand to give him support and, at the same time, to get support from this man who could only blink his eyes and cry.

Still out of body, Hillary heard the head doctor say, "I think we're going to have to give up. His heart rhythm has flat lined, and it's been more than twenty minutes. Even if his heart starts, there'll be a great deal of brain damage. This isn't the way a person would want to live."

These were perhaps the last words he would hear. Hillary then reentered his body without any conscious sense.

Mo grabbed the cardiologist who was running the code and said, "Doctor, help him! You must do something!"

The cardiologist felt horrible but knew nothing else could be done. Henry, who had been doing CPR the whole time, needed hope. He recalled a story Hillary told him about his father, about the time they had played the game HORSE. He remembered that in the story Hillary spoke of his dad's ability to still compete despite having ALS. The senior doc had a drive and spunk that wouldn't allow him to give up.

Henry looked at the stone-faced, wheelchair-bound doctor squarely in the eyes and implored, "Doc."

The cardiologist looked up at the clock and said, "Stop CPR. Let's call it. Time of death, one twenty-one p.m."

CHAPTER 32

꘎

J ust as the cardiologist stopped CPR and announced the time of
death, at that exact instant a loud voice was heard—not a regu-
lar one but rather a computer-generated voice made by the senior
Hillary. Eyes to retinal scanner to computer, he said, "Do not give
up on this young man. He is my son, and he will not die."

Everyone in the room was shocked, yet some felt a tiny bit of
rekindled hope.

The new voice of the senior Dr. Chollet spoke, "Henry, give
him three milligrams of intracardiac epinephrine."

Henry jumped to attention and told the medical intern, "Begin
CPR now!" He looked at the mystified cardiologist and barked an
order to the nurse to give him three milligrams—and before he
could get out the word "epinephrine," she had given him a syringe
of epinephrine with a spinal needle. The world-class cardiologist

was beside himself and in shock over the chutzpah this third-year surgery resident showed.

Even though his friend and teacher already had been pronounced dead, Henry readied himself with the syringe of epinephrine and found the subxiphoid process, located at the bottom part of the sternum. Slightly to the right of it he angled his syringe at forty-five degrees, toward the tip of the left shoulder. Usually this procedure was performed to remove blood from around the heart, and the heart itself was not to be punctured. This time, however, Henry was charged with piercing the pericardium, along with the left ventricle, and injecting the three milligrams of epinephrine. Without difficulty Henry popped the syringe through the pericardium and then into the ventricle, as documented by the return of blood into his syringe.

As he injected the epinephrine, he looked up at the heart monitor and flat-line rhythm, which meant clinical—and possibly biologic—death. He remembered, however, what his boss, the man who was on the table, once had said about the line between life and death. "Often we bump up against this line, and sometimes we go over the line, and that's when we most need hope, faith, and courage."

Feeling the passion of those words, Henry was barely able to contain his emotions. After injecting the epinephrine, he did CPR again and wouldn't give up. Beads of sweat and his own tears rolled down his cheeks and dripped onto the bare chest of his stricken friend.

Twenty seconds after the epinephrine injection, the heart monitor burped a single beep and a QRS complex. A few more seconds, and Henry heard another *beep*, then *beep*, *beep*, *beep*, *beep*, *beep*.

This was followed by Vfib. It wasn't a fine fibrillation; it was a coarse fibrillation that showed this heart still had something left. This caught the eye of the cardiologist, who felt like he was watching the movie *Animal House*.

The senior Hillary again used his computer-generated voice and confidently told Henry, "Shock him."

Henry grabbed the paddles and said, "Three hundred joules, please."

He placed the paddles—one over the sternum and the other over the left chest—and then, with a voice filled with hope, shouted, "Everyone clear," and discharged the paddles, delivering a shock. Henry thought of the irony; a shock had stopped Hillary's heart, and now a shock would hopefully restart it.

The ventricular fibrillation was shocked into flat line, but then after about ten seconds—what felt like an eternity—a single beep followed. There was a QRS complex followed by another QRS complex. A few seconds later another, then another, then another, then *beep*, *beep*, *beep*, *beep*, *beep*, *beep*, *beep*, *beep*...

A half minute later the nurse announced, "Doctor, blood pressure is one hundred over sixty."

Everyone cheered.

The cardiologist acknowledged that he had been premature in pronouncing this man dead. He accepted his mistake and jumped right back in. Henry was glad to turn things over, but like a bloodhound whose master was injured, he wouldn't leave Hillary's side.

Hillary was taken to ICU in critical condition, but he had a stable heart rate, blood pressure, and heart rhythm. After he arrived in the ICU, the nurses hooked him up to a respirator and started him on sedation in the form of Diprivan and little bit of Fentanyl. His good friend, Dr. Kassabian, was his pulmonary doctor. The cardiologist ordered several blood tests, including enzymes to see whether he had suffered a heart attack. A stat echocardiogram also was done, which looked remarkably good for someone who'd just had twenty minutes of CPR. Once Hillary had settled into the ICU, Mo and the senior Hillary were allowed to spend time with him.

The ICU room was big, with a monitor the size of a twenty-four-inch TV that displayed heart rhythm, oxygen saturation, and respiratory rate. Mo sat next to Hillary and held his left hand while the nurses hooked up Hillary, Sr.'s respirator and moved his left arm so that his hand could rest on top of his son's right hand. The sight of the father and son, both on respirators and unable to move, was nearly overwhelming for Mo. Once Hillary was stable, Henry left but came back from time to time to check on his friend.

Around 4:00 p.m., the chief of surgery came in as they wheeled in the young woman who had been shot in the heart. Her room was right across from Hillary's ICU room; they were only separated by a glass partition.

The chief told Mo and Hillary, "I've gone over all his tests and the echocardiogram, and as long as he wakes up, I think he'll make it." Speaking to the senior Hillary, and pointing through the glass to the next room, he said, "Your son saved this young woman's life, and right now she's very stable. She already has opened her eyes and is moving her arms and legs." He started to walk out but then turned around and added, "Doc, from what Henry said, you saved your son's life. Strong work—we may have to put you back on call. I need docs who have guts."

Around six o'clock, Maya came and took the elder Hillary home. Mo decided she would stay until ten or eleven. A little after eleven, around the time of the ICU nurse shift change, she felt one of Hillary's fingers move, then his entire hand. She looked at him, and he started to open his eyes. She raced to get the night ICU nurse, Melanie, who came in and witnessed the event as well.

Mo suddenly felt the pressure of the day finally catch up with her. She sat down and sobbed, saying, "I couldn't bear to lose him."

Trying to console her, Melanie extended her hand, which Mo accepted. The look on her face struck Melanie. It was obvious she had very deep feelings for Hillary.

Maureen kissed Hillary's hand and then kissed him on the cheek. The nurse encouraged her to go home so she could get some rest, but Mo pleaded, "Can't I sleep in the chair next to him?"

That night Melanie bent the rules and let Mo stay next to her man.

Throughout the night Hillary remained stable, and at 4:00 a.m. he was sent for a CAT scan of the brain. Other orders included more blood tests, an EKG, a chest X-ray, and another echocardiogram. The chest X-ray showed he had four broken ribs on the left side near the sternum. That was from Henry's CPR. At eight o'clock in the morning, Dr. Kassabian, the pulmonary doctor, came by, and the ICU nurse gave Hillary a sedation vacation, which meant all the sedatives were turned off to see how awake he was.

After five minutes, the Diprivan wore off completely, and Hillary opened his eyes. He was able to hold up two fingers when asked to. Dr. Kassabian checked the airway pressures and blood gas and thought Hillary could come off the respirator. He gave orders to Anna, the respiratory therapist, and they started a fast wean. Anna knew her job well and had worked with Dr. Chollet on numerous occasions. She particularly liked the way he treated his patients, along with the trust he had in her. Anna was more than a respiratory therapist. She was part coach, part psychiatrist, and a full-time nice person.

Anna told Mo, "Go home, change, and get some rest. It's my pleasure to take care of the doctor."

Over the next thirty-five minutes, with the coaching and encouragement of Anna, Hillary was weaned from the respirator, and by eighty-forty in the morning, he was off the vent. At nine o'clock, Mo returned after a one-hour break. She was amazed to see Hillary off the respirator—so happy that she told him she loved him and had been up all night praying.

"How do you feel?" she asked.

Hillary said, "I feel a little sore, but overall I don't feel too bad. I'm a little confused about exactly what happened, though."

Over the next half hour, Mo relayed the events that had transpired and how the cardiologist basically had given up and pronounced him dead. She added that his father and Henry had saved his life.

The ICU nurse came in and offered Hillary some clear liquids—apple juice, broth, and red Jell-O. Hillary sipped the apple juice, and given what he had been through, he thought it tasted wonderful. Dr. Kassabian came back to ICU after Hillary had come off the vent and told Mo he was satisfied with Hillary's progress. The chief of surgery came in and shook Hillary's hand. He said that the young woman who had been shot was doing fine, and by afternoon he was going get her off the vent.

After everyone had made rounds, Mo said, "Sweetie, after they took you to ICU, I picked up your scrubs from the floor of the trauma room, and this piece of paper fell out of your pocket."

Hillary didn't have a good memory of what had happened and felt confused because of a dream he had while his heart was stopped. "Go ahead, sweetie," he said. "Tell me what it says."

Mo opened the letter and read, "Dear Father Andrew, Hillary and I would be proud to have you at our wedding." The letter went on to describe Janet and Hillary and ended with "Respectfully, Janet Dingwall."

"Let me see that." Hillary read and reread the note. He paused afterward and felt an incredible revelation as he thought, *It all must be true. My memories of the past: New Orleans, Father Andrew, Sister Madeline, Father Solomon, Billy, Holy Cross, being a math teacher and a football coach.*

Mo asked Hillary about the letter, and he answered, "I think something very powerful has happened to me."

Hillary reached for Maureen and hugged her. She was so happy her "baby" was doing so well. After lunch she wanted him to get some rest and told him she would be back around dinnertime.

He fell asleep, and when he woke up, it was around two in the afternoon and Maya was sitting next to him. She picked up his hand, kissed it, and said, "Your father is so proud of you. Since yesterday he won't stop talking with his new voice. He even said he was thinking about going back to work part-time."

Both Maya and Hillary laughed. A few minutes later, Maya reached into her purse and pulled out a little round box and said, "This was given to your father at the time of his wedding, and now he wants to pass it on to you. He said you're a soldier of God, and this will help you through difficult times of decision and remind you what a soldier's duties are."

Hillary remembered the box but wasn't exactly sure how. He removed the top and turned it upside down and had a feeling of comfort as the coin fell into his outstretched hand. On one side there was a picture of the cosmos and on the other side a picture of Jesus as God.

As he held the coin once again, he felt inclusiveness for all peoples and faiths.

Hillary said, "Thank you, Maya. When I see my dad in a few days, I'll thank him also."

Maya left, and around four o'clock, physical therapy and occupational therapy came. They got Hillary out of bed and even helped him take a few steps. The nurse removed his Foley catheter and the central line that had been placed in his groin vein, and told him he would be transferred to a telemetry unit. Just as they were wheeling him to his new room, Mo came with some flowers and followed the transport team down the hallway, up two floors in the elevator to his new room.

As Hillary acclimated to his new room, Henry and Janelle visited for a few minutes. Hillary thanked both Henry and Janelle. "Thanks, guys, and thank you, Henry, for saving me, but next time, guy, be a little more gentle on the ribs."

They all laughed as Hillary pretended to be in pain when he touched the ribs on his left side.

Over the next few hours, Mo and Hillary talked about many things, including their future. After dinner, around seven o'clock, she could see Hillary's eyes were growing weary, so she said good night and gave him a kiss.

That night, as Hillary rested, he thought about how glad he was to be alive. His head was still in a bit of a whirlwind as he said his prayers, and his mind felt the memory and presence of Father Andrew, which made him wonder if he had multiple personalities.

For the time being, he figured he would take a "wait and see" approach and just go with the flow. The next morning, at around six, the cardiologist stopped by and said the heart monitor could be discontinued and that Hillary could be up as much as he wanted.

After his morning therapy, dressed in the pajamas Mo had brought, Hillary decided to take a walk. He felt a little tight and tender, but with the aid of a cane he was able to walk off the unit and take the elevator down to the first floor. Every fifteen or twenty feet, he leaned against the wall to rest for a bit.

Toward the front of the hospital there was a little garden, and Hillary peeked through the window, enjoying the morning sun. As he was finishing his view of the garden, he saw an orderly pushing a woman in a wheelchair about thirty yards away. This garden was close to the hospital entrance, where visitors came inside and signed in. Hillary looked at the woman. He could see she was a black woman.

A few minutes later, a much older black woman and a little boy came into view. The little boy couldn't have been older than five. He ran to the woman in the wheelchair, laid his head in her lap, and said in a loud voice, "Mommy."

Hillary knew this was the woman who had been shot in the chest and the little boy who had called 911. It was nice to see them reunited. Hillary felt a sense of pride but decided the worst thing he could do would be to walk up to them and overshadow their moment.

Taking the chance to reflect, he knew that being a doctor was, at times, a lonely existence. More often than not, his success was rewarded with a quiet celebration with himself.

Hillary smiled as the boy hugged and kissed his mother. A few minutes later, he walked back to his room and jotted down a few notes, and for the first time, he thought about going back to work. A little bored, he looked in the suitcase Mo had brought and again examined the round box that held the beautiful coin.

His mind wandered as he held the box, and as he moved the box from his right hand to his left, he felt the bottom move. *That's strange*, he thought, and then something popped into his mind— "Half a turn clockwise and one turn counterclockwise."

Hillary looked around his room to make sure he was alone.

"Clockwise and counterclockwise," he said out loud as he turned the bottom, and out popped a little drawer. Inside the drawer was a card.

Hillary laughed as he removed the card and read it. "Saint Hilary of Poitiers, Doctor of the Church." He closed his eyes and thought back to New Orleans and all that had happened, and then proclaimed, "It was all true!"

How cool, he thought. Then he decided this was something he should quietly celebrate—keep to himself—so he returned the card to the drawer and closed it. Hillary then wrote a note to himself.

Remember the past.

Live in the present.

Have an eye toward the future.

Be a good soldier.

Live with faith, hope, courage, and love.

CHAPTER 33

ᴄᴍᴍᴏ

D r. Kassabian visited at nine the next morning and surprised his friend. "Doc," he said, "today I'm going to let you go home."

Hillary was glad to be going home. Mo arrived at around nine thirty. To Hillary's eyes she looked beautiful; she wore a pastel sundress, sexy shoes, and a wide-brimmed hat. Excited, she came up to Hillary and hugged and kissed him.

"Sweetie," she said, "Dr. Kassabian will wheel you out front, and I'll pull the car around and we'll go home."

She winked at Dr. Kassabian as if something was up, but Hillary didn't take notice. As he gathered his things, he made sure he didn't forget anything. Dr. Kassabian brought in a wheelchair and said, "Sorry, Doc. Standard operating procedure. Everyone goes out in a wheelchair."

Smiling, Hillary sat down in the wheelchair and placed his suitcase on his lap. Then Dr. Kassabian wheeled him to the front of the hospital. They went through the sliding glass doors into the driveway area, and what Hillary saw next made him cry out. There were at least a hundred people from the hospital—doctors, nurses, orderlies, and people from housekeeping, along with Henry and Janelle. They all clapped as Dr. Kassabian wheeled Hillary toward Mo's car.

Mo was in the driver's seat of her little Mercedes, with the top down. Dr. Kassabian rolled Hillary right up to the passenger's side, where Henry already had opened the door.

Hillary stood and said, "Thank you all so much. Your support means everything to me."

Everyone clapped again, and Henry put his arm around his good friend and said, "Doc, for the next three weeks, you're on vacation. Then it's back to work."

Henry and Hillary hugged, and Hillary got into the car, fastened his seatbelt, and waved good-bye. He kissed Mo on the lips, and as they were driving out of the parking lot, he said, "Maureen, will you marry me?"

Mo slammed on the brakes, put the car in park, and threw her arms around him. Wincing from his cracked ribs, he awaited her answer.

"Yes, sweetie, I will."

The couple drove toward the beach on Pacific Coast Highway, heading up the coast to Santa Barbara, where they were going to stay at a little place Mo had read about.

CHARLES JACOB CHOLLET, HARVARD

GRADUATION PICTURE, 1887

"Professor Chollet met his death by an accidental discharge of his gun while he was out training some young dogs for hunting. No one was with him at the time of the accident, nor did anyone arrive until after he died. It seemed from his position near a fence that a rail had broken under his weight while he was crossing it and that he was thrown violently to the ground, causing his shotgun to discharge. He died from internal hemorrhage.

"He was well loved by all connected with the university and was held in high esteem as an instructor."

THE (MORGANTOWN, WEST VIRGINIA) NEW DOMINION.

WEDNESDAY, AUGUST 14, 1903

CHARLES AND OLIVIA'S BOYS, MICHAEL, AL, AND CHARLES

(LEFT TO RIGHT)

OLIVIA

ROSA

1900 US CENSUS, NINTH WARD, NEW ORLEANS

1900 US CENSUS, NINTH WARD, NEW ORLEANS

"United States Census, 1900," Olivia Olinde in household of Rosa Olinde, ED 72 Ward 9 New Rhodes town, Pointe Coupee, Louisiana, United States

Name:	Olivia Olinde
Titles & Terms:	
Event:	Census
Event Date:	1900
Event Place:	ED 72 Ward 9 New Rhodes town, Pointe Coupee, Louisiana, United States
Birth Date:	Oct 1873
Birthplace:	Louisiana
Relationship to Head of Household:	Daughter
Father's Birthplace:	Louisiana
Mother's Birthplace:	Louisiana
Race or Color (Standardized):	Black
Gender:	Female
Marital Status:	Single
Years Married:	
Estimated Marriage Year:	
Mother How Many Children:	
Number Living Children:	
Immigration Year:	
Page:	3
Sheet Letter:	B
Family Number:	55
Reference Number:	53
Film Number:	1240577
Digital Folder Number:	004120192
Image Number:	00593

Household		Gender	Age	Birthplace
Head	Rosa Olinde	F	50	Louisiana
Daughter	Christine Olinde	F	34	Louisiana
Daughter	Olivia Olinde	F	27	Louisiana
Daughter	Marie Olinde	F	21	Louisiana
Daughter	Lorenza Olinde	F	20	Louisiana
Daughter	Resencda Olinde	F	14	Louisiana

"United States Census, 1900," Rosa Olinde, ED 72 Ward 9 New Rhodes town, Pointe Coupee, Louisiana, United States

Name:	Rosa Olinde
Titles & Terms:	
Event:	Census
Event Date:	1900
Event Place:	ED 72 Ward 9 New Rhodes town, Pointe Coupee, Louisiana, United States
Birth Date:	May 1850
Birthplace:	Louisiana
Relationship to Head of Household:	Head
Father's Birthplace:	Louisiana
Mother's Birthplace:	Louisiana
Race or Color (Standardized):	Black
Gender:	Female
Marital Status:	Widowed
Years Married:	
Estimated Marriage Year:	
Mother How Many Children:	7
Number Living Children:	7
Immigration Year:	
Page:	3
Sheet Letter:	B
Family Number:	55
Reference Number:	51
Film Number:	1240577
Digital Folder Number:	004120192
Image Number:	00593

Household		Gender	Age	Birthplace
Head	Rosa Olinde	F	50	Louisiana
Daughter	Christine Olinde	F	34	Louisiana
Daughter	Olivia Olinde	F	27	Louisiana
Daughter	Marie Olinde	F	21	Louisiana
Daughter	Lorenza Olinde	F	20	Louisiana
Daughter	Resencda Olinde	F	14	Louisiana

**HILLARY AGE 12; HELPING AT HOLY CROSS CHURCH,
1938 CHRISTMAS**

HILLARY, SOPHMORE IN HIGH SCHOOL AT HOLY CROSS (#11)

March 19, 1946

Hillary Cholett
Holy Cross High School
New Orleans, La.

Dear Hillary:

Tony Cash informs us that you are interested in
attending Notre Dame. If this is so, we would
like very much to hear from you.

Kindly give us a brief outline of your scholastic
record and your athletic experience. It is also
necessary to let us know about your draft status.

Your promptness in replying will be greatly appreciated.

Cordially,

Hugh Devore

Hugh Devore

ds

F. W. THOMAS
ATHLETIC DIRECTOR AND
FOOTBALL COACH

June 14, 1945

Mr. Hilary Schollet
3112 Cleveland Ave.
New Orleans, La.

Dear Hilary:

I have heard from my good friend Eddie Reed in New Orleans
who tells me that you are very much interested in going to
College. I have heard about your football ability from
him and through the newspapers.

I wonder if you would be interested in coming up here and
spending a day or two with us, at our expense. I would
like very much for you to see the Campus and discuss further
plans with you.

Hoping to hear from you soon, I remain,

Sincerely yours

FRANK W. THOMAS

FWT:MS.
P. S. I have also written Joseph Ernst. I hope you boys
can come up here together.

OFFICE OF THE
REGISTRAR

July 6th,
1 9 4 5.

Mr. Hillary Anthony Chollet
3112 Cleveland Ave.
New Orleans 19, La.

My dear Mr. Chollet:

      Acknowledging receipt of your
certificate of record as a graduate of the Holy
Cross High School, Class of May 1945, I take pleasure
in informing you that the Admission Committee has
approved the same for admission to the Scientific-
Medical Course.

      Registration day was July 5th,
and you should report as soon as possible for regis-
tration.

      Yours very truly,

      Florence W. Toppino
      Mrs. F. W. Toppino
      Assistant Registrar

L

Copy: Brother Owen, C. S.C., Principal
      Holy Cross High School

HILLARY AT CORNELL (1945-1950)

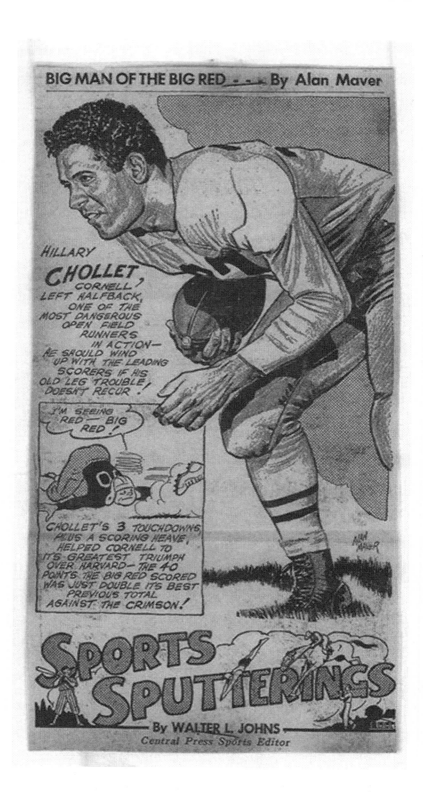

OFFICIAL BASKETBALL PROGRAM

Published by the Cornell University Athletic Association

Printed by Art Craft of Ithaca, Inc.

Vol. 6, No. 13

February 26, 1949

Harvard and Hillary

Harvard had better watch out tonight. The Cambridge Johns are facing a fellow who has raised havoc with them in sports during the course of the last year. He is our Captain Hillary Chollet.

Tonight Hillary plays his last game for Cornell home folks against the visiting Crimson and if he could duplicate the performance he put on in Syracuse Wednesday it would be a fitting climax to his court career. Over in the Coliseum against Syracuse, he set and broke more records than one could reasonably expect from any individual and he did it in a losing cause.

A shy, likeable guy, Hillary poured in 37 points. He stole the ball from the Orange backboard and raced downcourt to score all by himself. He dropped 19 of 23 free throws which indicated Syracuse's strategy in stopping him by fouling and when he broke the Coliseum scoring records he received a tremendous ovation from the Orange partisans—and that's another record.

Harvard Coach Bill Barclay will have a definite defensive pattern set up to stop Hillary tonight but Lew Andreas of Syracuse did too. It didn't work. Lew first put one man and then another on the New Orleans lad and finally wound up with about three covering Hillary and

the other two working on his teammates who just couldn't buy a basket.

In the Boston Garden last winter Chollet had a field day and his performance was so outstanding the Boston sportswriters awarded him a place on their all-garden team. The year before Chollet was an all Ivy League choice. Not only has he plagued the Crimson on the court but Hillary has

Captain Hillary Chollet

been a bother to the Cambridge football team. Last fall he scored three touchdowns against them and he'll be back next season for further tries. But his basketball eligibility is ending soon which is the reason why you'll be watching him in a Cornell jersey and short pants for the last time tonight.

Hapless Harvard, still striving for its first win of the year in the Eastern Intercollegiate League, has been acting tough lately losing to good teams by

scant margins. In an earlier meeting against Cornell the visitors dropped a 51 to 42 decision but they did better against Columbia and Pennsylvania than the Big Red.

Neither team is going anywhere in the Ivy loop race this season for Harvard is imbedded in the cellar and Cornell hasn't a chance for its customary bridesmaid's role with a four and four record. The Big Red youngsters with Sophomore Paul Gerwin and such other performers as Tom Turner, Jack Rose and Mike Schaffer will be favored in this final contest of the basketball season at home.

Harvard will throw the very able athlete Chip Gannon and some others against them but Gannon, a versatile three letterman, is rated as the best of the Cambridge crew. Walter McCurdy, a prolific scorer, is to be watched also along with towering John Rockwell and the even taller Bill Prior.

The visitors have a 6-foot-5 front line with Prior, Rockwell and Sophomore Ed Smith and are expected to use it in the event Chollet makes his farewell to the home folks a copy of the Syracuse spree.

Series Record

Series started: 1901-02
Cornell 34, Harvard 26
Harvard 24, Cornell 20

Longest winning streak:
Cornell (5 games)
1941-42 through 1st game, 1948-49
(Teams did not play 1943-44 through 1945-46)

Highest Harvard score:
Harvard 59, Cornell 71 (1947-48)

Highest Cornell score:
Cornell 71, Harvard 59 (1947-48)

1947-48 scores:
Cornell 57, Harvard 45 (Ithaca)
Cornell 71, Harvard 59 (Boston)

This season: Cornell 21, Harvard 13

EASTERN INTERCOLLEGIATE LEAGUE

	Won	Lost
Columbia	6	1
Yale	7	2
Princeton	5	3
Cornell	4	4
Penn	4	4
Dartmouth	2	7
Harvard	0	7

Cornell Schedule

43	GETTYSBURG 49
67	BUFFALO 44
57	COLGATE 48
47	NIAGARA 54
57	*YALE 44
56	Michigan State 45
47	Illinois 71
50	John Carroll 62
64	Utah 52
33	Canisius 56
44	SYRACUSE 49
51	*Harvard 42
64	CANISIUS 36
47	*Pennsylvania 34
40	*Yale 55
57	*DARTMOUTH 51
52	MUHLENBERG 54
43	*PENNSYLVANIA 45
59	*PRINCETON 44
71	Colgate 69
50	*COLUMBIA 58
53	Syracuse 70

Feb. 26—*HARVARD at Ithaca
Mar. 5—*Princeton at Princeton
Mar. 7—*Columbia at New York
Mar. 12—*Dartmouth at Hanover

*Eastern Intercollegiate League games.

HILLARY AND CORNELL COACH LEFTY JAMES, 1949

HILLARY WORKING AS A HOSPITAL ORDERLY WITH KIDS WITH POLIO, 1949

DR. DAY RECEIVES FOOTBALL

HILLARY CHOLLET '50, (left) is shown handing DR. and MRS. EDMUND EZRA DAY the football used during the Cornell-Penn game as a gift from the student body. The scene was part of the Bailey Hall reception Thursday honoring Dr. Day.

HILLARY HANDING THE GAME BALL TO DR. AND
MRS. EZRA DAY, 1949

HILLARY INJURED DURING ARMY-CORNELL GAME, 1948

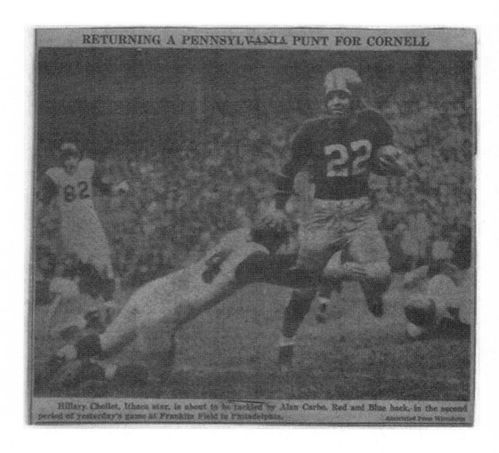

RETURNING A PENNSYLVANIA PUNT FOR CORNELL

Hillary Chollet, Ithaca star, is about to be tackled by Alan Carbo, Red and Blue back, in the second period of yesterday's game at Franklin Field in Philadelphia.
Associated Press Wirephoto

MISS DINGWALL WED TO DR. H. A. CHOLLET

Special to The New York Times.

ITHACA, N. Y., June 14—Miss Janet Dingwall, daughter of Dr. and Mrs. Andrew Dingwall of Upper Montclair, N. J., and Westerly, R. I., was married here today to Dr. Hillary Anthony Chollet, son of Mrs. Alfred Chollet of Buffalo.

The ceremony was performed in Our Lady's Chapel at the Newman Oratory on the campus of Cornell University by Msgr. Donald M. Cleary. There was a reception at the Statler Club.

The bride's mother was matron of honor. Anthony Gaccione was best man. After a wedding trip, the couple will reside in New York, where the bridegroom is serving his interneship at Bellevue Hospital.

Mrs. Chollet was graduated from the Walnut Hill School, Natick, Mass., and the College of Home Economics at Cornell. She is a junior member of the Pen and Brush Club in New York and assistant fashion director of the National Cotton Council of America in New York.

Her father is a fellow of the New York Academy of Sciences and a fellow of the Royal Institute of Chemistry of Britain. Her mother, a member of the faculty of Hunter College, was formerly a director of the University of Minnesota theatre.

The bridegroom was graduated from Cornell, where he was a member of the varsity football team and was captain of the basketball team. Dr. Chollet is also an alumnus of the Cornell Medical College in New York.

The New York Times
Published: June 15, 1955
Copyright © The New York Times

287

The Big Red went 8-1 in 1948, led by halfback Hillary Chollet, in the opinion of some the greatest all-around athlete Cornell has ever produced.

As a prep school star in New Orleans, Chollet was assiduously recruited by both Louisiana State and Tulane. When Chollet chose Tulane, someone leaked to the newspapers that LSU had not wanted him anyway because he had Negro blood. The Chollets were Cajun, but because of the rumors the family was shunned socially and even made to feel unwelcome in their church. Tulane quietly suggested that Chollet might find it difficult to go there. Fortunately, a Tulane booster knew that Chollet hoped to study medicine and recommended Cornell.

From *Football: The Ivy League Origins of an American Obsession*, by Mark F. Bernstein, 2001

The Cornell Daily Sun

Keith R. Johnson '56 Digital Archive

Catholic to Preach at Sage; First Time in Univ. History [ARTICLE]

Cornell Daily Sun, Volume LXXXI, Issue 57, 11 December 1964, Page 7

Catholic to Preach at Sage; First Time in Univ. History

The unprecedented participation of a Catholic priest in the Sage Chapel services Sunday reflects the change in Catholic attitudes resulting from the Vatican Council, according to the Msgr. Donald M. Cleary, who was University Catholic Chaplain for 25 years and now pastor of St. Catherine's Church in Ithaca. He will speak on "God, Man and Environment." Although Catholic clergymen have been invited to participate in the non-denominational services in the past, it has been impossible for them to accept. Msgr. Cleary said, "The Council has given the Catholic clergy greater freedom to participate in services of this nature." The first appearance of a Catholic priest at Sage Chapel is one more evidence of the disappearance of animosity and the advent of a friendlier spirit between different religious traditions. He added, "We hope that a new tradition is established so that in the future Catholic theologians will be invited to preach at the Sage Chapel services and that they will accept these invitations."

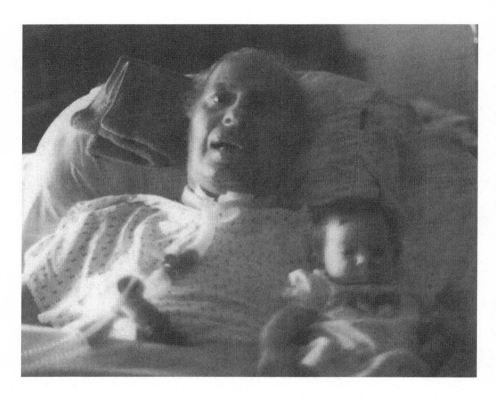

HILLARY AND GRANDDAUGHTER ARIEL

Made in the USA
Columbia, SC
22 April 2022

59328087R00178